AF260702

MAKE ME FORGET

THE WALKER BROTHERS, BOOK 4

AMANDA ADAMS

MAKE ME FORGET:

Derek Walker is in Vegas for his brother's wedding.

A bachelor party. A little gambling. A week of fun with his brothers.

What could possibly go wrong?

He could fall in love, that's what.

He just might meet his match…but when her past comes calling, it will challenge everything he thinks he knows about family, loyalty…and love.

Copyright 2017 Amanda Adams
Make Me Forget: The Walker Brothers, Book 4
Cover design Copyright 2017 by eBook Indie Covers

Literary Work, First Edition. August 2017
Copyright 2017 by Amanda Adams
Published By Tydbyts Media
All rights reserved.

This book is a work of fiction. Names, people, places and events are completely a product of the author's imagination or used fictitiously. Any resemblance to any persons, living or dead, is completely coincidental.

PROLOGUE

*D*erek Walker pulled into the lawyer's driveway and turned off the engine to stare at the icicles and snow hanging from the giant blue spruce next to the drive. It looked like a giant Christmas tree, the snow and ice glittered in the bright Colorado sunshine like a million tiny diamonds. It was beautiful, and tragic, and reminded him of the only two women who had ever mattered to him. Both dead.

The pain was like a pitchfork shoved through his chest, ice cold and sharp as broken glass.

Derek looked at himself in the rear-view mirror, into the dark brown eyes that reminded him so much of his grandmother. He took several deep breaths as he stared, making sure he had his shit together before he got out of the car. Today was going to hurt, a lot, and he needed to be strong for his brothers. They depended on him to be tough, to keep his shit together. If he lost it, they would fall like bricks behind him.

The steering wheel squeaked as he unknowingly attempted to strangle the life out of it while he paused to steady his resolve and wrap the pain up in layers of mind-numbing logic. He exhaled with relief when his brother, Mitchell, younger by six months, pulled onto the driveway behind him in his cherry-red sports car. Their youngest brother Jake, already here, had parked his white truck on the street smack in the middle of a pile of snow the plows had left behind. The sight made him smile. Jake was all country; because what else was a giant pile of snow on the side of the road for, if not to park on?

Relieved to be able to move, to stop thinking, stop *remembering*, Derek opened the door of his SUV, stepped out and slammed it closed behind him. He was dressed, as usual, in black, a stark contrast to Mitchell's dress pants and sport coat. Mitchell used to raise hell, but had gone over to the dark side, the respectable side. A fucking surgeon who wore dress pants and a jacket to work every day. But when it came to women, they were both in the same boat; not interested in anything long term. Hell, that seemed to be the running theme among the four brothers. They'd all been adopted from hellholes and saved by the mother whose memory they were all here to honor.

Losing her ripped them all to pieces but in this moment, Derek needed to play his role. He straightened his shoulders, breathed in deep and twisted the kinks out of his neck. Time to do what he always did, take care of his family. He could hurt later. He could rage and race his Ducati Monster around curved mountain roads like a demon chased him. Later. Right now he had one job…to keep his shit together. To be an anchor for his brothers. That was all.

Mitchell nodded at Derek and, as always, his brother fell in step beside him as they made their way up the driveway to the front door. Neither of them spoke. They didn't need to. They both knew why they were here, and it sucked.

Mrs. Klasky opened the door in a pair of navy-blue pants and an oversized, cream-colored sweater. She was pushing eighty, but had a sparkle in her eyes and a practical manner that Derek appreciated. Derek didn't play games. Life was too short for that shit. If he hated someone, or wanted them in bed, they knew about it.

"Come in. Come in. Jake is already here." She motioned them inside and Derek stepped into the hallway with Mitchell a couple steps behind. When Derek looked over his shoulder at her, she smiled. "Still as handsome as ever, I see. Straight on back to the kitchen, boys. I made lemonade. And I have cookies, Derek. Your favorite."

Derek felt his face heat and Mitchell, as usual, aware of everything going on around him, ran some much needed interference. Mrs. Klasky had always pampered Derek the most, had a sweet spot for him a mile wide.

Which was nice, in an uncomfortable way. And he knew, without a doubt, that Mitchell would give him shit about it later. Mitchell's grinning reply confirmed that. "Thanks, Mrs. Klasky. We can't wait to have some of your cookies."

Derek coughed into his hand and took the opportunity to hit Mitchell on the back of the head, hard, as they followed her past a wall filled with family photos and sepia-toned portraits of the Klasky family's ancestors. Shag green carpet ran wall to wall where it met with ancient wood paneling that had probably been installed in the seventies. And an old song tip-toed through the outskirts of Derek's mind, though he couldn't remember the title. He had a vague recollection of John Lennon writing a song about burning some girl's awful wood paneling, and he could understand why.

Jake sat in his usual spot at the Klasky kitchen table, in the hardwood oak chair closest to the twenty-year-old sofa covered with a hideous paisley print.

Derek hadn't been in the house in years. It still looked the same. Felt the same. Smelled the same. Mitchell smacked Jake on the back by way of greeting. His baby brother was the youngest, but the little fucker had outgrown them all by about five inches and a good fifty pounds. Put a pair of cowboy boots and a hat on the kid and he looked like a linebacker for the Dallas Cowboys. Except he was too pretty for that. And too damn soft-hearted. Jake still lived on the family ranch, taking care of horses and doing his cowboy shit. He tossed around hundred-pound hay bales like they were cracker boxes. And as the baby, Jake never passed up an opportunity to rub their noses in the fact that he could kick every single one of his older brothers' asses.

Derek appreciated his brother's love of the country life. They'd all lived on the ranch after the adoption, and the quiet had soothed his anger in a way nothing else could have. But after a while, the isolation became too hard to bear. There was too much space and too much time to think about the past.

He took a deep breath as the scents of cookies, lemonade and pine-scented cleaner surrounded him.

"Here you go, boys." Mrs. Klasky set a glass of lemonade in front of each of the boys. Derek knew exactly what it would taste like and his mouth began to water before the drink even reached his mouth. He remembered being draped across that ugly-ass couch waiting for his mother and Mrs. Klasky to finish their small-town gossip on more than one occasion, pretending not to listen, but absorbing every word. He knew who was dating whom, who got caught cheating, driving drunk, fighting in the bars. He always listened. It was a hard earned skill that had kept him alive when he was younger.

"Thanks." Mitchell, always the gentleman, spoke for both of them.

The doorbell chimed and Mrs. Klasky excused herself. "That'll be Chance." Mrs. Klasky disappeared again and came back with his brother Chance, the newly blooded attorney just a year out of law school. Chance rolled in wearing a suit and tie, and an odd sense of pride twisted in Derek's chest. His brothers were all okay. They'd made something of themselves, had overcome their shit pasts. Derek knew his mother deserved all of the credit, but he took some small satisfaction for the heads he'd beat in, the bullies he'd threatened, the heat he'd taken off his brothers, shit they never knew about.

His brothers were everything. Family was everything to Derek. His grandmother had taught him that before she died. Not his worthless father, who took off before Derek was born. Not his abusive, alcoholic mother who made his life a living hell. But he'd been held when he was small, he'd been loved. And he knew, despite all the shit he had survived, he'd been lucky.

"Chance." Derek got up from his seat at the end of the table and wrapped Chance up in a hug.

"Hey, loser." After a quick hug, Chance patted Derek on the shoulder. Jake and Mitchell took their turns greeting their law dog brother. Even given the situation, Derek's smile widened as the joy of having the brothers together in one place emanated from his chest and flooded his head like a jolt of adrenaline. Mrs. Klasky's husband, also an attorney, had invited them here for something regarding their late mother's estate. They'd all assumed everything was taken care of, so this little get-together was a bit awkward.

"Late to the party, as usual." Jake grabbed Chance and lifted him off the floor as if his brother were a little girl. The two youngest, Jake and Chance, were close and Mitchell grinned at Jake's antics. It was good to be together. Always good.

"And you still smell like cow patties and hay bales." Chance chuckled but Jake wasn't going to take the insult lying down.

"Damn right, brother. And you smell like you had your ass wiped by a bathroom attendant with a perfumed moist towelette. You turnin' into one of those metrosexual, city boys?" Jake set Chance down and Mitchell answered for him.

"Naw, man. That would be me." Mitchell grinned and grabbed Chance around the shoulders.

Chance stood there in his suit, and as usual, he was the only one in a tie. Even Mr. Klasky, their mother's eighty-year-old attorney, was in khakis and a golf shirt.

"Now that you're all here, we can begin." Mr. Klasky rolled in a small television with the old-fashioned VCR combo. Jake kicked out a chair with his foot and Chance sat in it, tugging on his tie to loosen the noose around his neck. He'd just started working at a well-respected law firm in the city. Poor bastard worked almost as many hours as Mitchell did as a second-year surgical resident.

They all thanked Mrs. Klasky as she served them a tray of chocolate chip cookies, just as she'd been doing since they were in grade school. She gave Derek an extra pat on the cheek as she passed him and Mitchell hid his grin behind his hand. Derek kicked him under the table.

Mrs. Klasky smiled as she walked back to the counter and stood, leaning against the wall. Jake offered her his seat, but she shooed him away. "You boys are going to want to be sitting down for this."

"All due respect, Mr. Klasky, but Mother's estate was taken care of months ago when she first got sick." Chance spoke up and Derek watched Mrs. Klasky's expression as something close to anticipation flashed behind her eyes. What the hell were his mother's old friends up to?

"Yes. Yes. I know." The older man bent over, looking for an outlet in the wall so he could plug in the dinosaur of a television.

"Then why are we here?" Chance's gaze darted from Mr. Klasky, who had finally found an outlet and was shoving the electrical prongs into it, to his wife, who glowered at him with a raised eyebrow until he added, "Sir."

Mr. Klasky stood up and rubbed his hands together like he couldn't wait to spring a huge surprise on them. Derek shifted in his seat and thrummed his fingers on the table. Derek *hated* surprises.

"Well, boys, I promised your momma that I would get you all together today, six weeks to the day after she passed. God rest her soul."

"But why? Everything's been handled." Chance leaned forward, in total lawyer mode.

"Not everything." Mrs. Klasky pulled four envelopes from her apron pocket. Each looked like it would hold an oversized birthday card. She walked to the table and handed one to each of them. "Don't open them yet. You have to watch the video first."

Chance's envelope was green. Jake's was plain white. Mitchell's was a faded red. And Derek inspected the card in his hand, the envelope a bright, sunny yellow with his mother's cursive handwriting on the front.

Fuck. Leave it to their mother to pull this shit from beyond the grave. She always had been two or three steps ahead of her boys. Always. That was how she'd straightened them out. Their mother always knew what was going on with her sons, sometimes even before they knew themselves.

"Holy hell." Jake leaned back in his seat and started tapping his cowboy hat against his knee, which was code for an impending volcanic eruption.

Mr. Klasky shoved an old VHS tape into the player and the fuzzy screen went black for a few seconds. The old tape began to make a whirring noise as it played.

Mitchell sat with a grin on his face and his elbows on the table. Derek ignored them all as his mom's voice echoed through the crappy television speakers. The video feed made an odd knocking sound as the image of his mother leaning forward to check the camera came on. Satisfied, she nodded then sat down in a chair positioned so her face would fill the small screen.

She looked young and healthy, strong. Seeing her look like that hurt, reminded him of how horrible she'd looked when the cancer ate her alive from the inside out.

Shit.

"Hello, my precious boys. I'm going to make this tape and give it to Mr. Klasky just in case something happens to me. I don't plan on going anywhere, but if I do, I want you boys to know I loved you more than anything and I was always proud, every single day, to be your mother."

Jake sniffed and turned his head away. Mitchell leaned forward with a sigh and Chance was holding his breath. Derek froze, afraid to move, afraid to leak the smallest reaction. If he started to allow the pain out, it would explode and never stop, rip him to pieces easy as Shrapnel slicing through paper.

"You boys know how much I always pushed you to follow your own hearts. Follow your dreams, I say. Well, I've been thinking about this a lot this past year. Derek is fourteen now, and I see it happening already.

"Life is going to get ahold of you boys, and drain your dreams right out of you. I know. The real world is hard and unforgiving. Boys don't get to have dreams anymore. They have to be men. The world is going to expect you to be hard. And I know you can be hard as nails. All of you. I know where you came from. You were born into a hard world. I tried to show you a different life, but I'm afraid. I'm afraid

you're going to grow up and forget who you really are. I don't want you to forget your dreams.

"*So, I did something a little crazy. Maybe you'll remember, maybe you won't, but on my birthday this year, I asked each of you to write a very special card—*"

His mother's laughter filled the quiet kitchen. That laugh. No matter how messed up he'd get in his head, that laugh had always made him feel like everything was going to be okay.

"*I'm going to ask Mr. Klasky to hold on to these cards for a while. Someday, I'll die. Maybe I'll be ninety, maybe not, but if I'm gone and you need reminding, he's going to remind you of who you really are.*"

Her expression changed from mischievous and full of herself to solemn and serious. She leaned forward until her face filled the *entire* screen.

"*I love you. Each and every one. And you each made a promise to me, all those years ago. And dead or not, I expect you to keep it.*"

She threw her head back and laughed, the sparkle back in her eye. Oh, she knew she'd won. She was gone and her boys couldn't even argue with her now. No push back, no whining, no denial. She had them all by the shorthairs and she'd known it, all those years ago when she made the recording, she'd known her boys would keep their promises, because that was how she'd raised them.

"*Dead or not. How's that for a good one? I love you. Don't forget who you were born to be. Open your cards now.*"

Read them. And above all, remember why you wrote them. Keep your promises. I love you, and you know I'll be watching."

They all sat in stunned silence and Derek stared at the card in his hand. He knew what was in it. He didn't even need to open it. He remembered every word. Looking up to inspect each of his brothers' faces, he recognized the stunned denial on each of them. They were all in the same boat, it seemed. Derek hoped they'd each written something epic in their cards, something fun and crazy and totally wild. The words he'd written that day were burned into his brain like a brand, and he'd lived them every single day since.

There was no big reveal for him inside the envelope, no dream to chase. He'd never dreamed, not like that, not like his brothers had.

As they filed out a few minutes later, Mrs. Klasky pulled him aside in the kitchen. "Your mom wanted me to tell you especially, Derek, to be sure to open your card."

He looked down into her kind, wrinkle-lined eyes. "Why? I know what I wrote. I remember."

She nodded and patted him on the shoulder. "Yes, dear. But you don't know what she wrote back to you."

1
___

ne Year Later

CHANCE LEANED BACK IN HIS CHAIR, LIFTING THE FRONT two legs off the wood floor and shaking his head to shout over the noise. "No. No fucking bachelor party, you assholes."

Derek sipped on his beer and hid his grin behind the glass as Mitchell stirred up trouble. "Too late, little brother. All the fancy electronic invitations have already gone out."

"You're a bastard." Chance popped a loaded nacho chip into his mouth and grimaced as Jake's rumbling laughter carried over the top of the loud music the bar's DJ pumped through the speakers. The Walker brothers had gathered for their once a month ritual and Friday night bullshitting session, but this time was special. Baby brother Chance was getting married to the love of his life in three short weeks. In Las Vegas.

"Yeah, well, blame Tyler. The Castillo trio was in on it, too." Mitchell's new brothers-in-law were all young, single, and spent most of their time raising hell in the hugely successful band, Castillo. They had signed with the same record label Chance's fiancée, Erin had, and so they were all melding into one gigantic, musical family.

"Yeah? Well, tell that little shit Tyler, if there's a stripper trying to sit on my face, I'm going to knock his head into next week. You know I hate that shit."

Mitchell's grin was not at all reassuring as he made quick work of a basket full of hot wings and french fries drenched in ranch dressing. The doctor ate like a fourteen year old, no matter how much his wife, Jessica, pampered him with home cooked meals and the most delicious muffins Derek had ever tasted.

Jake, the big cowboy, beamed with pride from across the table. He'd beaten them all to the altar, dragging Claire in front of a preacher one short month after they got back together. Derek watched a big grin spread across the quiet, country boy's face, and couldn't let him escape the fray. "Jake, you're glowing like a girl."

"Claire gets back tomorrow." Jake waggled his eyebrows with a grin. "Let's just say… I don't plan on either of us sleeping for at least a week."

Jake's wife, Claire was an archeologist and had just spent the past two months on a dig somewhere in Italy, in a small village that got gobbled up by the same volcano that wiped out Pompeii. Hercules or something like that. Derek had no idea, and didn't care. All he cared about was the shit-eating grin on his baby brother's face. If his brothers were happy, then everything was cool.

Mitchell finished off the last hot wing and tossed it in the paper-lined basket. "I don't know how you stand it, man. Being away from her for so long."

"Jesus, Mitchell, you sound like you're completely pussy-whipped. Have some pride." Derek stole a french fry and pointed it at his brother.

"So Jessica has me by the balls, I don't care who knows it." Mitchell and Jake were both sporting gold wedding bands on their left hands and Mitchell's first child, a son, was due in a couple of months. His brothers looked good, content in a way Derek had never seen them before, and couldn't relate to. Inside, he still felt raw and edgy, hunted. There was no reason for it, no logical explanation or psychological voodoo he could use to get rid of it. He was always on guard, always waiting for trouble, ready to fight. He'd been this way his whole life, and didn't know how to turn it off. Most days, Derek didn't mind the aggression that fermented inside him like an infection, but sitting here with his contented brothers made the contrast that much stronger and harder to explain. They'd survived hell, all four of them. So why did Derek feel like the only one still riding the razor's edge?

With a sigh, he took another sip of beer. He'd taken it on himself to take care of his brothers years ago. His demons were his own, and there was no need to cry like a baby about it. He was all about family, and taking care of his little brothers. With Jake and Mitchell settled, he had two brothers down, one to go. Chance was the only one not legally married yet. Once his baby brother was off the market officially, maybe Derek could learn how to relax, stop playing big brother and watchdog all the time. Stop worrying. Stop waiting for the other shoe to drop.

Yeah, right.

"I'm damn sure ready for her to come home," Jake said.

"We all know what you want." Chance's teasing laughter forced a loud rumble that shook Jake's shoulders and a rush of pink colored the blond giant's cheeks. Mitchell didn't miss a beat.

"You get really good at phone sex, or what?"

Jake choked on his beer and Derek laughed out loud. Jake lowered his glass and looked Derek square in the eye. "I don't know what you're laughing at. You're in a shit ton of trouble and don't even know it."

Confused, Derek tilted his head and scowled. "What are you talking about?"

Mitchell and Chance both snickered behind their hands and wouldn't look Derek in the eye. Jake, however, stared him down as if he was the butt of a joke, with Derek the only one who didn't know the punch line.

"What the fuck are you talking about, Jake?"

Mitchell leaned back, a huge grin on his lips. Chance studied his beer with intense interest, an amused grin appearing and disappearing from his face. Jake, however, crossed his arms over his massive chest and smiled ear to ear. Derek was ready to punch him.

"The Walker women seem to think you need a wife."

Derek choked and Mitchell leaned forward to pound him on the back much harder than necessary. "What?"

Chance stopped fighting the urge and laughed. "They have each selected a female acquaintance they think would be perfect for you. They're going to stalk you, Derek. Every single one of the ladies will be armed with personal information and will be gunning for you." Chance paused, then burst out laughing once more. "They assigned one of their friends as your date for each event leading up to the wedding. They wrote a fucking schedule. It's going to be like your own personal version of *The Bachelor* TV show."

"Oh, shit. Are you kidding me?" Derek looked to Mitchell for confirmation. His closest brother shrugged.

"Poor Derek." Mitchell, the surgeon and soon-to-be-father, patted Derek's hand like Derek was a two year old throwing a tantrum. "You shouldn't be surprised. You know women love that matchmaker shit. And you,

Mr. Bad-Boy Biker, are a challenge they simply can't resist."

Derek rubbed his brow, a sudden and violent headache looming. "Please tell me this is some kind of twisted joke. A schedule?" He looked from brother to brother, meeting each of their sympathetic expressions in turn and trying not to feel sick. "Why didn't you idiots stop them?"

When they all looked at him with blank, helpless expressions, Derek knew the answer. "You three have got to grow some balls. Tell your women no once in a while."

Mitchell's laughter was so carefree, Derek didn't have the heart to tease him for it. "Right. I worked too hard to get Jessica to say yes, to ruin her fun." Mitchell's green eyes were so happy, Derek knew he was screwed. He wasn't going to get an ounce of help from any of these lovesick idiots.

Chance finished him off. "Besides, this should be fun to watch."

Derek leaned back in his chair and faced his three, smirking younger brothers. "You guys are dicks."

Mitchell popped a french fry into his mouth. "Learned from the master."

With a sigh, Derek shook his head. "All right. Seriously. Is there any way, any way at all that I can get your women to keep their noses out of my personal life?"

Jake sipped his beer. "Yeah, you can try to convince

them that you've fallen in love and bring a woman to the wedding. You have two weeks."

Derek scowled. "I'm not going."

"You're the best man, dumbass." Chance's smile was a mile wide.

2

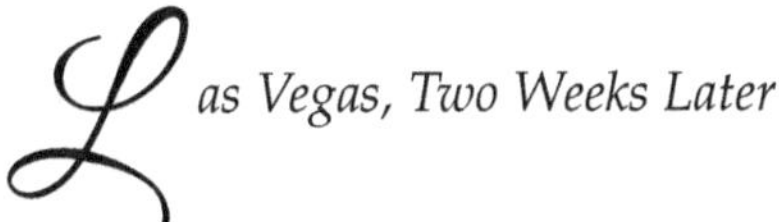

as Vegas, Two Weeks Later

LAURA GEORGE TRIED HER BEST TO GET LOST IN THE CHAOS and noise of the enormous tradeshow floor, the tingle running up and down her spine all the proof she needed that Benny's psychotic brother had followed her.

She walked along, admiring the stunning custom work done by the finest chop shops, motorcycle clubs, bike shops and individuals in the country. Every custom bike shop worth a damn was here, as well as the big name manufacturers like Harley Davidson and Ducati. Scanning the list on the program book, she frowned when she didn't see her favorite, Walker Custom, on the list. Last year, they'd shown up with a customized Ducati Monster that had blown her mind. She would have given her left leg to ride it, but had been forced to settle for taking her trusty, eight-year-old Yamaha out on a nearly suicidal high-speed run through the canyons.

But there'd be no more riding for a while. Her flight left first thing tomorrow for Denver. The ticket and five grand in cash in her purse all she had until the trial was over. She was leaving town and staying low. Her return plane ticket was in her purse as well, a one-way back to Vegas the day before she was due in court to face down a cold-blooded killer.

The carryon sized black suitcase she pulled along behind her five inch Valentino ankle strap heels contained all she could salvage of her life here until Benny got put on ice in the state pen. The rest of her belongings, from her designer shoe collection, racing leathers, toolbox, and the few personal things she'd managed to keep growing up, were in a storage unit on the north side of town. She didn't have time to rent a truck, find a place and try to relocate. The trial wasn't for almost six weeks, and Laura knew, if she stayed in Vegas another forty-eight hours, she'd be dead.

Her ex-boss, Benny, was sixty years old and not considered enough of a threat for her to be given police protection. As a small time crook, he wasn't mafia or a mega-millionaire. He wasn't connected. No, Benny was just a low-life, greedy asshole who'd killed a man, and done it right in front of her. And he happened to have a slightly older brother, named Richard, who'd spent his life cleaning up Benny's messes. Right now, *she* was the mess.

Like she needed more bullshit to deal with.

Pulling her small case along behind her, she walked to the display area of her second favorite bike shop and admired their work. The sight of so many bikes, the smell of oil and tires, made her so homesick for her dad's garage her throat swelled and her eyes burned. He'd taught her everything he knew about working on bikes, and being here made her feel like he was still with her somehow, watching over her from wherever he was now. Heaven or hell, she had no idea. He hadn't been much of a nurturer, and he'd dragged her all over the country as easily as she was dragging the suitcase behind her, but he'd taught her about bikes, and he'd shown her the freedom that could only be found flying down the highway with the wind stealing her breath and the rumble of a powerful engine between her legs. He'd been a shit father, but at least he'd given her that.

As she admired a particularly beautiful customized Triumph, two men walked up next to her, admiring the same. One was tall and lean, good-looking with dark brown hair and green eyes. He had a wedding band on his left hand and his cursory glance at the bike let her know he wasn't the reason the two were here.

The other man, however, made her heart race. He was a couple inches shorter, with hair so dark it looked almost black. His eyes were a rich brown the color of her favorite chocolate and intensely focused as he knelt down and ran his fingers along the shiny, black gas tank like he was touching the finest jewel. Both men wore black suits and white shirts, like they'd just come from a wedding, or a funeral. On the taller man, it fit, the ease of his stance and comfortable way he rested his hands inside the jacket pockets testament that he was used to the attire. But on his sexy friend, the suit was a mockery, like a tiger wearing a top hat. His motions were restless and edgy as he tugged on the collar revealing the top edge of a tattoo she really would have liked to see more of. Hell, he was gorgeous. She wanted to see more than just his tattoo.

The tall one spoke first, standing over the other with a bored look on his face. "We should get back, Derek. They're probably looking for you by now."

Laura stepped marginally closer, not wanting to miss a word, the same curiosity that had made her the star of a murder trial obviously still alive and well, despite being hunted. She would have rolled her eyes at her own stupidity, but the hottie, Derek, answered his friend.

"Don't talk to me right now. I can't go back there."

Curiosity piqued, Laura stayed put, pretending to read her program book.

Green eyes laughed. "You have to. Who's going to give the toast?"

Ah, so a wedding then? Laura turned the page.

"I don't fucking care, Mitchell. Let Jake do it. I can't take any more."

Mitchell burst out laughing at his friend's predicament and Laura had to hold back a smirk of her own at the sound of Mitchell's laughter. "Listen, big brother, I know the women are driving you crazy, but it's just one more night. Be strong."

So, they were brothers? Even more interesting. And who was Jake?

Derek stood and Laura moved to stand behind him, discreetly, of course, and not because she couldn't keep her eyes off his ass.

"Listen, I can't do it. I can't go back there tonight. They're all crazy." Derek rubbed his hand along the back of his neck and Laura actually felt sorry for him. He sounded so defeated.

"They're not crazy, Derek. They're single."

That made her burst out laughing, but she covered it the best she could with violent coughing sounds. Too late, Derek's attention flickered to her. In two seconds flat he'd inspected her from the tip of her head, down her hot pink and black striped dress to the tips of her hot pink toes. His gaze lingered on her suitcase for a brief second before meeting her gaze.

All the air left her lungs and she couldn't breathe as she looked into a pair of the sexiest bedroom eyes she'd ever seen. His black eyelashes could put mascara models to shame. His shoulders filled out that suit like he'd been poured into it, and his hands looked rough and calloused from hard work, just the way she liked them.

God, he was *haaaawt*. Intense. The total bad-boy, and she had to remind herself that she was leaving in fourteen hours, on an airplane, going to another state. She was going to go to Denver, find a job as a mechanic and lay low until the trial. End of story.

When he turned back around to his brother, she shivered but kept listening. This was too juicy to pass up.

"They're crazy, Mitchell. They're nice women, I'm sure, but there's just no fucking way I can deal with that. I can't believe Jessica thought I'd go for that yoga nut."

Mitchell chuckled as Derek continued, "She dragged me down to the hot tub last night. So, I thought, okay, let's see where this goes. But the second we're in the water she tries to bend me into a pretzel and then tells me we were married in a past life as peasants in ancient Rome."

"So, an ex-wife, huh?" Mitchell's smirk held absolutely no sympathy and Laura felt rooted to the spot. So, this was what it felt like to have a brother, someone to share things with, someone who would give you a hard time, tease you, but still love you in the end. She felt like a voyeur, watching and longing for something she'd never had, and never would.

Derek actually chuckled this time. "Yeah, right." He ran his hand along one of the motorcycles that she had already admired and she couldn't tear her gaze from the soft slide of his hand over the molded chrome. He caressed the bike as if she were a lover and he were soothing her, getting to know her before he took her for a hard, fast ride…

"The other two were just as bad." Derek didn't look at his brother as he explained, instead tilting his head so he could get a closer look at all of the engine components. "Erin's rocker friend turned into a clinging, whiny mess the second we were alone. She may look like a hard ass, goth rocker, which, by the way, I have no idea why Erin would think that was my kind of woman…"

Mitchell interrupted, "No one knows your type, Derek. I haven't seen you with a date in years, other than one night stands you pick up in a bar."

"Maybe that is my type."

Mitchell snorted. "Bullshit, man. I know you better than that."

"Fuck you."

"What about the other one? She seemed nice."

Derek stood and walked to the next bike. Trying to remain invisible, Laura scooted a few steps in that direction. This conversation was classic, too good to give up.

"She's nice. Absolutely. Preschool teacher. Sweet as can be."

"And? What's the problem with that?"

Laura bit her lip. *Yeah, what was wrong with that?*

Women could be nice. Sweet. What was sweeter than a freaking preschool teacher? If a girl like that couldn't land a man, there was no hope for wildcard women like Laura.

Derek was close to the bike, but looked at his brother when he answered. "Fifteen minutes into dinner she informs me that she wants to live in Boulder, have four kids, and tells me what their names will be. She also warned me that she always wanted the Golden Retriever's name to be Sampson."

Mitchell shrugged. "So, married with four kids and a dog in the under thirty minutes?"

"Exactly."

"And I thought Jake was a fast mover."

Derek walked around and slapped Mitchell on the back. "He knew Claire for years. You only knew Jessica a month. You're the wild one in the family now. You have officially stolen my crown."

"When it's right, it's right." Mitchell shrugged, but the happiness in his smile was intriguing and Laura found herself wishing she could meet this Jessica. "But I'm guessing you don't want to walk back over there and face the firing squad?"

"Not really."

"We have to go back, Derek. Chance is probably looking for us already. You know they're going to want to take more pictures."

"I know." Derek and Mitchell stood shoulder to shoulder almost directly across from Laura, where she continued to read her program book as if her life depended on it, turning pages every few seconds so it looked like she was actually seeing what she was staring at. Derek cleared his throat. "I don't suppose you'd be interested in going with me as my personal bodyguard?"

Laura kept her head down, waiting for whoever Derek had spoken to, to answer him.

When the silence stretched, she lifted her chin cautiously to find Derek staring straight at her, waiting. When he had her undivided attention, he asked her again. "Well? What do you say?"

Laura froze like a deer in the headlights. "Me?"

3

"Yes. You." His grin was infectious and spread from his face to Mitchell's before she felt her own lips curve up at the edges. "I need a hot date to keep the crazies away."

"I don't know." He thought she was hot? Butterflies raced in her stomach. She took a deep breath and scanned the crowd, certain she'd spy Benny's vile brother at any moment. She needed to get the hell out of here, and leaving with these two suddenly sounded a hell of a lot better than leaving alone. If she were lucky, she'd slip out of here and Benny's brother would lose track of her completely. She studied Derek for a minute. "Tell me your top three, favorite bikes of all time."

"Is this a test?"

"Yes."

He was smiling now, his eyes sparkling with her challenge. "A test of what, exactly?"

She shrugged, unwilling to enlighten him. She could tell a lot about a man by the kind of bike he liked, and found she really wanted to know his answer. Was he a hard ass or weekend warrior? Did her prefer speed or comfort? Did he like a roaring set of pipes or the quiet hum of a stealthy engine? "Just answer the question."

"If I do, you'll agree to be my bodyguard for the evening?" Derek walked over to her, never breaking eye contact. A shiver raced over her spine as he neared, the bike on the showroom floor the only thing between them.

"Maybe, if your answers don't suck."

She saw the laughter in his eyes, but he buried if fast. His gaze was intense, interested, and she refused to show weakness, refused to look away. With her super-woman high heels on, she could almost look him straight in the eye. Oh, hell yeah. She grew up around this crowd, knew how this dominance game was played, and she wasn't about to back down and give him the advantage.

"Triumph T120 Bonneville."

She nodded. "1959. Agreed." She crossed her arms now, impressed but trying not to show it. He knew his stuff. Not just a pretty face then, and that thought increased her interest by about a thousand percent. "Next?"

"R 80 G/S."

So, he was a fan of European bikes. And off-roading. Still, he'd mentioned two of the most iconic, famous bikes there were. Those two bikes were on almost every Top Ten list out there on the internet. "Too easy. What's your final choice, and it better be good."

"A Ducati Monster 1200 S."

"What color?" It didn't matter, but she wanted to know. In the brand new fantasy stirring to life in the back of her mind…

"Black."

"Of course." She bit her lower lip with indecision as he watched her, waiting for her to make the next move. Should she go with him to the wedding? Hang on his arm and smile and flirt and pretend to be a princess? She had on her princess clothes, suddenly thankful her father had always insisted they dress their best when traveling. He'd taught her that the finer the clothes, the better the service, and she'd seen firsthand that dear old dad was right, at least about that.

His brother stepped up beside them and stole her attention from Derek. She blinked for the first time in a long time when Mitchell spoke. "We have to get back."

Derek looked to her and held out his hand. "You going to save me or what?"

She couldn't do it, not without telling him the score. "I'm leaving town in a few hours. This was supposed to be my last stop."

Derek looked from her suitcase back to her face. "We're flying out tomorrow, too." He walked around and reached for the extended handle of her suitcase. "Come with me. Save me from dog-name negotiations."

"Will there be food?"

Mitchell grinned at her from where he stood, hands in his pockets and an amused look on his face. "Tons of food. Steak. Lobster. Champagne."

"Beer?" God, she could really use an ice-cold beer right about now.

"As much as you can drink," Derek promised.

She laughed and handed over her suitcase handle. "That's about two." When he held out his arm like a gentleman she took one final look around, made sure Benny's homicidal brother was nowhere in sight, and took his arm with a smile, the strong feel of his bulging biceps impossible to miss through the thin material of his suit. "Okay. I will protect you from the crazy preschool teacher, Derek, in exchange for two beers, dinner, and one slow dance."

She threw on that last request on a whim. Why? She had no clue, but he was gorgeous, dressed to kill, and her date to a wedding where she would not know a single soul. She didn't want to sit around all night watching everyone else dance. She'd done enough of that in high school.

"Deal. What's your name?"

"Laura."

"Just Laura?"

She thought about it for a few seconds and nodded. "Yes, just Laura. And I don't want to know your last name, either."

"Why not?"

She sighed dramatically. "Because we're only going to be together for a few hours, and I don't want to be tempted to google you later."

He chuckled and handed her case to Mitchell, who took it with an overly exaggerated roll of his eyes.

"You think you'd google me? Try to track me down?" He escorted her along the concrete showroom floor, heading toward an exit.

"Like a bloodhound." She tilted her head and rested it on his shoulder, looking up at him with the widest, most innocent cow-eyes she could manage. She then batted her eyelashes for added effect. "Didn't I mention I'm a homicidal stalker?"

His smile made butterflies swirl in her stomach. "No. I think you left that one, tiny, little detail off your official bodyguard resume."

Lifting her head, she grinned. "Well, you have now officially been warned." Pulling her phone from her purse, she opened her car app and confirmed her location. Sure, she was crazy enough to go to a wedding reception with two complete strangers who *seemed* like decent guys, but she wasn't a complete idiot. "Where are we headed? I'll call a car."

"You won't need that." Derek sighed. "I didn't run far. The reception is in one of the ballrooms in the hotel across the street."

———

Three hours later Derek slid onto the barstool next to his bodyguard, whose feminine presence had worked like a charm at keeping the crazies away, and stole a sip of her beer. It was warm, and only half gone, despite the fact that she'd been carrying it around for almost two hours.

"Hey!" Her mock protest fell on deaf ears and he took a second drink before setting it down in front of her and signaling the bartender.

"That's not even close to cold. You want something else?"

"Sure."

They ordered two iced sodas and sipped on them as he watched all three of his brothers, and their wives, slow dancing. Chance's bride, Erin, looked fantastic in a simple dress that draped her curves and hung to the floor in a gentle glide. The material looked soft, like white rose pedals. Derek liked it, not too fancy, not a ton of sequins and shit to snag on everything, but still beautiful. Her shoulders were bare and her blond hair was up in some fancy hairstyle it seemed the women in magazines always had when they got married, which meant Chance couldn't seem to keep his lips from wandering up and down the side of her neck and shoulder as the danced. Derek would have teased his brother, told the bastard to get a room, but he knew for a fact they already had the bridal suite reserved for tonight and were leaving tomorrow for a honeymoon in Hawaii.

A few feet away his baby brother, Jake, towered over his wife. Claire was back from Italy and they were wrapped around each other so tightly it looked like they'd melted into one person. Claire's bare feet were actually on top of Jake's cowboy boots, her feet not even touching the floor as they swayed to the music.

Mitchell had his wife, Jessica, turned so her back was pressed to his chest as his hands caressed the baby bump that would soon grow to be little Thomas, his future nephew. Jessica's eyes were closed and her head was turned, tucked neatly beneath Mitchell's jaw. She was practically glowing.

His brothers all looked content, their hard edges gone, the hunger he'd always seen in their eyes, the fear, was gone, too.

"Let me guess, you're the oldest?"

"That obvious?" He turned to find her studying him with her dark eyes

Laura's grin was infectious and he couldn't help but wonder about her. Who was she? Where did she come from? And how did she know so much about bikes?

She took a sip of her soda and he stared as her full lips seemed to linger on the ice-cold rim of the glass. "Always the tough guy on the playground beating up all the other kids if they even looked sideways at one of your little brothers?" Laura's soft question wasn't really a question, more a statement, and suddenly he felt like he was being judged, analyzed. *Seen.* He squirmed on his seat and turned his attention to his drink.

"Yes. I guess so." The silence stretched and he risked looking at her again.

She was smiling down into her drink, her look a little bit sad, perhaps wistful. "You were all lucky."

He wasn't going to argue, not about that, and this wasn't the time to drag out the sad story of what their lives had been *before* their mother found them, adopted them. "You don't have any siblings?"

She shook her head. "Does a father with the mentality of a six-year old count?"

"Nope."

"Well, in that case, no. It was just me and my dad."

He glanced at her for a second, wanting to ask more questions about her life, but not willing to pry. After all, there was no future with this woman. She was his bodyguard for the night, her only purpose to keep the crazies at bay. She wasn't his real date, his girlfriend. Hell, he didn't even know her last name. He had a thousand questions and no right to ask any of them.

But that didn't stop him from wanting to ask. But he wanted a lot of things he shouldn't at the moment. He wanted to touch her skin. He wanted to kiss her. He wanted to know what put the shadows behind her beautiful amber eyes. Most of all, he wanted to know how she knew so much about bikes. He'd never met a woman who gave a damn. Even his mother, who had come by his shop at least once a month just to say hello, never did understand his fascination with riding.

But something about Laura was wild as well. From

the hot pink dress with the black racing stripe that outlined her curves to the sexy as hell high heels, everything about her was high octane. Black hair. Full lips. The way her gaze darted to the corners as if shadows chased her. Everything about her fascinated him.

She had slender arms but yet there was still some definition in them, the gentle outline of the muscles in her forearms one he'd seen before. Her hands would be strong, strong enough to pull back on the throttle of a bike for hours of riding, or on his cock for...

"Hello? Earth to Derek." Laura lifted her glass of cola and melting ice cubes in salute. "You still with me?"

"Yeah." As an answer, it sucked, but with her looking straight at him it was the best he could do. He could tell she worked out a lot. He always liked a girl who respected her body enough to take good care of it. She was spunky and vibrant, not at all shy. She held his gaze, eyebrows raised, and waited for him to get his shit together. "Sorry. I was thinking."

That made her smile and she might as well have gutted him. Everything and everyone else in the room faded away until he felt like he was alone with her, the only two people in the world.

She was petite, and he immediately felt the need to protect her, keep her close and beat the crap out of any guy who looked at her. Which was not exactly his style. He didn't do the jealous boyfriend gig. She had dark, wavy hair the color of his favorite black coffee and it fell halfway down her back in a thick mane he ached to sink his fingers into. Her skin was a silky smooth mocha not much different than his own. But her golden brown eyes were more like a tiger's than a human. She looked surreal, magical. Like a fairy tale come to life.

For the first time since his mother died, he wanted to impress a woman, be a perfect gentleman. Her posture as she sat there holding her drink was almost tired, as if she needed a pick me up, a boost of energy to get through the rest of the evening.

He had invited her to come to the wedding, so she deserved some attention. He got the feeling that when it had just been her and her childlike, irresponsible father, she had grown used to not getting much. That her father had been the first man to break her heart shouldn't matter, but for some reason he had no desire to examine, he felt compelled to ease the hurt he sensed behind her smile

"I believe I promised you a dance."

4

———

He tried to look casual and nonchalant as he dared a glance at her lips. He wanted a kiss. He wanted more. But for now, he'd settle for holding her and swaying to some bullshit eighties ballad. He stood and held out his hand to her but shrugged to make it seem like it didn't matter either way. He'd never admit the painful longing to feel her tiny frame pressed up against him.

She flicked her beautiful eyes in his direction, blinked shyly and placed her small hand in his. "Yes, you did."

He helped her up and laced his fingers with hers, moving her slowly over to the dance floor. Candles lined the walls and dozens of overhead lanterns lit the room with a soft, intimate glow, making the already romantic vibe in the room even stronger. The night was winding down, the upbeat dance music over a couple hours ago. Now the deejay slowed the music to match the mood, playing songs that only offered the couples on the floor one option. Close. Slow. Perfect.

His brothers were grinning behind his back, but he ignored them as he pulled the only person in the room who mattered at the moment closer. She smelled like wildflowers and he pressed her to him, burying his nose in her hair as she melted into him like she was meant to be there. They swayed to the music and he curled her right hand into his left and held it tightly to his shoulder. His free hand he placed on the small of her back, enjoying her curves, her warmth, the way her softer body fused with his.

It was all too easy to imagine her naked and writhing with pleasure. To envision her long dark hair spread out on his pillow as she reached for him, begging him to take her.

But that was never going to happen. They had one night. No last names.

Unless he could convince her otherwise.

Pulling away, he peered into her eyes, searching for any interest there that she might have for him. She returned his gaze with desire in her eyes. She licked her full lips and he stared, wondering what the dark pink lipstick would taste like, what *she* would taste like.

"Thanks for being my bodyguard tonight," he whispered over the sound of the music as their bodies moved together.

"All those years of Ninja training finally came in handy." She put her arms around his waist and smiled.

"Yes, they did." On an impulse he leaned down and kissed her on the temple, lingering just enough to get a small taste of her skin. Big mistake. The more he had of her, the more he wanted. He wasn't used to having this feeling of longing or connection. There was something different about Laura, the mysterious woman headed out of town in the morning. He found himself wanting to know where she had been, where she was going. "Tell me your name? What if I want to google you?"

"No chance, Romeo," she grinned up at him and it drove him wild. But even as his body stirred, his protective instincts were screaming. This woman had secrets, and they weren't the happy kind.

"I'm very good at keeping secrets, Laura. You can trust me." She stiffened in his hold and he knew he'd hit a nerve. He didn't want to upset her, but he couldn't hold her, talk to her, look into her eyes and let it go. That wasn't part of his DNA. He took care of the people he cared about. And despite the fact that he didn't even know her last name, he was shocked to discover he cared. "Whatever you're running from, tell me. Let me help you."

Her hand lifted from his waist to cup the side of his face and he was the one who melted. Such a simple touch. So much power to ruin him. "You can't help me. Thank you, but you can't help me. Nothing can help but time." She traced his lower lip with her thumb, her gaze growing dark with the same desire he felt. "And dancing."

Cryptic response. Why had he expected anything else? But if he was only going to be with her for a few more hours, he wanted to make every second of it count.

"Then let's dance," he pressed her closer. The chemistry sizzling between them, and the electric heat from her skin as she held onto him made him feel drunk. Off kilter and out of control.

He thought about asking for permission to kiss her, warning her of his intention. But he didn't want to risk saying the wrong damn thing, not when he wanted to taste her more than he'd wanted anything in a long, long time.

Holding her gaze, he took his time, made his intention known. He gave her long seconds to push him away, turn her head, anything to deny him this kiss. She didn't move away, didn't stop him and the world faded around him as he closed his eyes and finally took her mouth.

He lifted both hands to her head, holding her close, devouring her as she opened to him. They weren't dancing, but he didn't care that his feet stopped moving. The music faded. Everything faded as he explored her, memorized her taste, the way her hands fisted in the back of his jacket, pulling him closer. She was pure fire in his arms, a wildfire burning out of control.

Laura tore her lips from his with a soft sigh and dropped her forehead to his shoulder. "This was a bad idea."

He wanted to argue, he really did, but he couldn't risk pushing her. She was ready to bolt, he could feel it in the tension in her shoulders, the way her body shuddered when he wrapped his arms around her to hold her close. For the first time in years he had absolutely no idea what to say. He always had the answers, was full of advice for his brothers. But with her he felt like he was walking the razor's edge. "I'm glad you're here."

She smiled, he felt the slight pressure of her cheek pressed to his chest. "Me too. That's the problem."

He didn't say another word for long minutes and noticed that most of the wedding crowd was gone. His brothers tapped him on the shoulder one by one as the next half hour wore on, taking their wives up to their hotel rooms. To bed.

Which was where he wanted Laura. In his bed. He was rock hard, his body humming with a strange energy he'd never felt before. He knew it wasn't the music or the candlelight. It was her. She was doing something to him. He'd hooked up with women before, but this felt different. Maybe it was because he knew the clock was ticking, the minutes slipping through his fingers just like she was about to.

When the deejay announced the final song, they both stilled. Laura lifted her head from his shoulder and looked up into his eyes. "I guess this is it. Our last dance."

No. He wasn't ready to give her up yet. He needed her name. If she walked away now, she'd haunt him for the rest of his life. He knew it the same way he knew everything else, gut instinct. "It doesn't have to be."

Her smile was sad. "Yes. I'm leaving in a few hours, Derek."

"Stay with me." Lifting a hand to the back of her head, he buried his fingers in her hair and gripped the back of her neck with just a hint of the turmoil that was raging through him at the thought of never seeing her again, never knowing her real name. "Stay."

Laura gasped at the pressure as he angled her chin up, their lips inches apart. When she licked her lips, he bit back a groan. He worried for a split second that this would be too much for her, too aggressive, too demanding, too fast. But her breathing came hard and fast and her eyes grew dark with desire. "I'm not going to sleep with you."

The next words flew out of his mouth before he could censor them. "I'm not asking you to. Just, don't go. Not yet."

Her smile was wistful and full of something he remembered all too well, the expectation that the person she was dealing with was going to disappoint her. "So, what? I go up to your hotel room with you, we cuddle and drink champagne and I fall asleep in your arms?" She raised a brow. "You really expect me to believe that? After that kiss?"

"What kiss? I don't know what you're talking about." It was a gamble to be sure, but he had to try to charm her. Nothing else was working. And he couldn't lose her after just a few hours together. He didn't understand the urgency he was feeling, the way his heart pounded or his lungs labored for air. All he knew was he couldn't let her walk away. "I promise I won't make any moves. And I promise I'll let you go in the morning."

"I assume you have a room in this hotel?" she asked.

His heart skipped a beat as he studied her face for a hint of doubt. He saw nothing but loneliness and an indescribable need that matched his own. It had been a long time since he'd wanted to have a woman all to himself. He'd had neither the interest nor the occasion. But with Laura, all that changed in an instant. "Yes. A suite."

Lifting herself up on tiptoe to kiss him, she pressed her lips to his softly, the touch gentle. "Then let's go."

———

LAURA RAN HER HANDS OVER THE LEATHER LOVE SEAT IN the living room of Derek's posh hotel suite. She made her way to him and placed her hands on his biceps—squeezed them. Damn, those were huge. She wondered how chiseled and cut he looked underneath his suit jacket.

She cocked her head to the side and gazed up at him with a smile, while at the same time reaching her slender arms up around his neck.

She didn't know him well, but something about being pressed up against him felt so right, so natural that she didn't resist the temptation. Her small suitcase was next to the door and the bright lights of the strip were right outside the windows, calling her.

There was no way she could stay in this room—with him—and not do something stupid. So there was only one solution.

"Let's go."

"Go? Go where?" Derek asked.

Releasing him, she twirled around, arms in the air. This is *Vegas.* Let's go. There's an eleven o'clock show at the Lexor. I want to go see the Bellagio fountains one more time before I leave. There are slot machines and dancers and….just, come on. Live a little." She walked to the door, purse over her shoulder. "You coming? Or you going to sit in here feeling sorry for yourself all night?"

"I don't feel sorry for myself."

"Um-hmm." Grinning now, she let the door swing closed and walked over to a bottle of champagne she found sitting in half-melted ice. She popped the cork and poured two glasses before taking one to where he stood rooted like an oak tree in the middle of his suite, looking lost. "I know all the signs, Derek."

5

"**W**hat signs?" He was watching her through hooded eyes and hadn't taken a drink.

"Dark, brooding older brothers. Always watching over everyone else, never worried about his own happiness. Eternal sacrifice. Doom and gloom."

"That's bullshit, Laura. You don't know anything about me."

"I know enough." Lifting her glass, she held his gaze. "Here's to us. To right now. To no regrets."

They clinked glasses and she was relieved when he took a sip. But she knew the look in his eyes. He wanted her. Problem was, she wanted him too. And if they stayed here, inside this intimate little bubble with a king sized bed in the next room, she'd give in to temptation. She'd seduce him, and she'd regret it. She didn't do casual hook-ups, not for years. She's slept with enough

Hollywood wannabes and egomaniacs to last her a lifetime. Derek was special. He was real.

This was real, and she didn't want to pollute the waters with a one-night stand and a lifetime of regret. This night was pure magic, and she wanted to keep it that way, a precious jewel she could take out and look at over and over again.

The sliding glass door leading out to the balcony was opened all the way, letting a cool, soft breeze into the room. The drapes by the ends of the door billowed and flowed like dancing scarves in the wind.

"Oh wow, it's a full moon tonight," Laura pointed in observation.

"Things can get wild under a full moon." Derek winked at her.

"Only if you're a werewolf."

Derek chuckled and the darkness she'd seen in his eyes was gone. He carried a lot of pain, and she couldn't stop herself from trying to make him smile. "And are you?"

"What?"

"A werewolf."

"I'll never admit it." Walking out onto the balcony, she held her champagne flute and leaned on her elbows. He joined her and they looked down over the Las Vegas strip for a few minutes in silence. Millions of lights flashed, cars honked, pedestrians lined the sidewalks in a steady stream of humanity that looked like a river of ants moving far below them. The city pulsed with life, with possibilities. With danger.

"Let's go, Derek."

"Where do you want to go?"

"Everywhere." If she kept moving she never had to think about how lonely she was, how she had no friends, no family, no roots. "I'm a leaf in the wind."

"Now who's feeling sorry for herself?" The words were hard but his voice was soft, an invitation to confide in him. Trust him. Tell him…everything.

Standing straight, she finished off her champagne in one shot and turned to face him. "Exactly. Which I hate. So let's get the hell out of here and go have some fun."

"It's after eleven."

"I don't care. The fountains run until midnight."

"We won't make it in time."

"We can take a taxi." She was not giving in, not on this. Her options were either get out there and distract herself, or jump on Derek and strip his clothes off before he could protest. There was no in-between for her. None. She'd always been an all-or-nothing kind of girl. She'd tried to change, she really had, but she'd learned the trait from her dad, and when someone's doing stunt driving, half-measures get them killed.

He wrapped his arm around her waist and pulled her close, studying her carefully. "Kiss me, and then I'll take you wherever you want to go." He was observant, she'd give him that. But she was a master at hiding. "Promise?"

"Yes."

She stepped into him and lifted her chin. "Deal."

He lowered his head and she closed her eyes in anticipation. When his lips finally pressed to hers it wasn't at all what she'd expected.

She'd been waiting for a duel of tongues, a hot and heavy and completely dominant conquest of her mouth. She'd braced for it, prepared to enjoy him…but resist.

Instead, his kiss was gentle. And not a single kiss, a continuous assault, one kiss after another. There was nothing to resist, no force of will or command in his caress. Every touch of his lips was in invitation that she had no will to deny. He was like gravity and she was falling.

He broke her in less than a minute, her hands buried in his hair, her body pressed tightly to his. She moaned and tugged him down to her, demanding entry to his mouth. She was the aggressor, out of her mind with want.

Instead of giving her what she wanted, he pulled back and stared down at her with a storm of emotion in his eyes. "You are a dangerous woman."

"I'm a werewolf. What do you expect?"

His grin loosened the iron fist that had wrapped around her heart. "I thought you weren't supposed to admit it."

"You tortured it out of me."

His hands fisted in her dress at the small of her back

and he pulled her closer. "Is that what you call it? Torture?"

"Yes." And it was torture, wanting him. "You make me forget everything else." *Everything* else. Like knowing it could never work between them, that he was a stranger. And the fact that she was being hunted by a two-bit creep. Or the even sadder reality that she was leaving town in exactly seven and a half hours and had to come back to testify in a murder trial in six weeks. Derek lived in another state, had a perfect family. People he loved. People to protect from people with problems like hers. This thing between them was a disaster waiting to happen. "So let's go."

He didn't protest this time when she walked to the door. Instead he entwined their fingers and walked with her. Fifteen minutes later she stood in front of the fountains with Derek behind her, arms wrapped around her waist, his head resting on top of her shoulder like they'd been a couple forever. Like they belonged.

She took him shopping, and for ice cream. They played slots and people watched and went to a late-night comedy show where she laughed too easily and he watched her a bit too much.

Three hours later, she couldn't take it. She'd been up for over twenty-four hours, organizing her things, getting packed and putting the rest of her meager belongings in storage. As much as she didn't want the night to end, her body betrayed her.

Derek took one look at her, hailed a cab and ignored her protests as the car took them back to his hotel.

When they reached his room, he walked her to the bathroom, took of his jacket, dress shirt and the t-shirt beneath, which he handed to her. "You can't sleep in a dress and heels. Here."

She took the offered shirt, ignored his bare chest and shoulders the best she could and closed the door. It was a relief to kick off the heels and get out of the dress. She left her bra and panties on and slid the soft cotton over her head. It fell to mid-thigh. Perfectly acceptable. And it smelled like him.

Lifting the collar of the shirt to her nose she inhaled deeply and closed her eyes. God, yes. He smelled wonderful. Musk and some kind of woodsy cologne and all Derek.

She took care of business, hung up her dress and made her way back into the bedroom to find him waiting. He'd left his pants on, but he'd pulled down the sheets and made room for her next to him. "Come here. You're asleep on your feet."

She didn't bother warning him off. He was in protector mode and she knew with absolute certainty that he wouldn't make a move on her, which was a relief and, at the same time, disappointing. Which was just confusing as hell and she was too tired to think about it.

Besides, there wasn't anything she'd ever wanted in

her life more than she wanted to curl up in the safety of his arms and go to sleep.

Crawling in next to him, she rested her head on his shoulder and threw her arm over his waist. It felt too good to be true, perfect, but she ignored the warning bells going off in her head. She'd set the alarm on her phone hours ago and knew it would wake her in time to go to the airport, so she was free to enjoy the moment. They lay there together, intertwined in the sheets. Before she knew it, she was drifting off into a deep and much needed sleep.

She woke a few hours later. It was dark and quiet in the room and she could feel Derek's arm propped up over her breasts. Her alarm was going off on her phone, the one she set to wake her in time to make it to the airport.

She winced, hoping it wouldn't wake him. She leaned over and fumbled in the dark to turn the alarm off. He only stirred, rolled over and remained asleep. She breathed out a sigh of relief.

She got dressed in the cascading shadows of the moonlight. She gave Derek one last longing glance. She hated to leave in the wee hours of the morning like this, wished things were different and she could stick around. But she remembered him mentioning he was headed home tomorrow, too. This thing between them was just one night, a good time, nothing more. She could accept that and move on. At least she could leave here with the memory of being with him burned into her brain forever.

There was no way she could start a relationship with the looming murder trial and Benny's brother trying to kill her. Sticking around would just put Derek and his beautiful family in danger. Besides, she was nothing, an orphan drifter with no family and no real home. Derek had his shit together. It was obvious from the confident way he carried himself. What would he want with an unemployed stunt rider and sometimes Vegas show dancer? Staying would be irrational and stupid. She considered leaving Derek a note, but thought it was best to just slip away like a ghost in the night.

Derek seemed like a truly decent human being—which, in her experience, was a rarity. She didn't need to drag him into all the drama of her life. With one more glance in his direction; she watched in fascination as his chest rose and fell peacefully in the quiet. She inspected the lines of the tattoos she wished she had time to learn, to explore with her tongue. If he were really hers, she could spend hours learning the intricate designs, tasting his skin, tracing the patterns with her fingers. She ached to touch him one more time but didn't dare. If he woke, she might not have the will to do the right thing and leave him out of her messed up life.

Rethinking the note, she found a small pad of hotel paper on the desk and grabbed a pen. Scribbling a quick message, she signed it with just an L and left it on the pillow next to him. He could read that later.

She looked from her suitcase to the door and back at his face. He looked like heaven on Earth lying in that bed with his shirt off and the sheet down around his hips. The sight made her eyes burn as the weeks and months of anxiety and pain came flooding back into her body. With him, she'd been at peace for the first time in months. He'd felt like home, like lazy smiles and slow kisses and knowing someone always had her back. The feeling was absurd, she'd only known him a few hours, but the urge to crawl back under the sheets and cuddle up beside him was so strong it made her nauseous to fight her body's demands. But she realized she wouldn't be able to live with herself if she sneaked out on him. That wasn't her style. And Derek? He deserved better than that. But she was running out of time. She just needed to suck it up, say goodbye and get out of here before she missed her flight.

Sitting on the side of the bed right next to him, she made a production of putting on her heels. When Derek stirred, she leaned down and kissed him on the lips. "I have to go."

"No." He reached for her and she let him pull her down to his chest for a hug. This was the last time she'd ever be in his arms, and she wasn't about to deny herself.

"My flight leaves in two hours. I'm already running late. I can't miss it." Turning her head, she kissed his chest and wished she'd had more time to get to know him. Wished she didn't have a homicidal maniac chasing her around town. Mostly, she wished Derek lived here and she'd met him months ago.

His hands threaded in her hair, soothing her, massaging her scalp until her eyes drifted closed. God, if she could figure out how he did that to her, what kind of magical formula he used to get under her skin, she could bottle it and make millions. "Where are you going?" he asked.

Blinking slowly, she roused herself enough to push away from him. Hands on either side of his head, she leaned over him, her dark hair a curtain locking them into a very intimate space. "Somewhere far, far away."

"Why?"

The blunt question threw her off guard. Maybe the secrets were too heavy, or maybe it was just *him*. Maybe she felt the need to talk because she knew she'd never see him again and, for once in her life, showing weakness wouldn't come back to bite her in the ass. Whatever it was, the truth came tumbling out of her before she could stop it. "I have to hide. I witnessed a murder, and the trial is next month. The murderer's asshole brother is trying to kill me so I can't testify. I have to leave town until the trial starts."

"What?" The relaxed blur behind Derek's dark eyes vanished in an instant.

Yeah. That shocked reaction was about what she expected. And the patch of hair sticking straight up on Derek's head was, in a word, adorable. "You wake up cute."

"What?" He reached for her again, wrapping his hands around her biceps. "Say that again."

She knew what he meant, but she chose to ignore the order. She'd already told him too much. It was time to cut bait and run unless she wanted to drag him into her chaos, and he was too good of a man for that. Her life was a mess, dangerous and nomadic. Derek had brothers, sisters, a new nephew on the way. He did *not* need her brand of madness. "You wake up cute."

Reaching for the patch of hair sticking up on the side of his head, she patted it down, leaned in and kissed him goodbye.

"I'm not cute, and you're not leaving until you explain."

Forehead pressed to his, eyes so close she had to concentrate to see him, she shook her head. "I have to go."

6

____

"No. What about witness protection or something? The police should be protecting you."

That made her laugh, the sound bitter. "Yeah, right. He's a two bit criminal, not a drug lord or mafia king. He's nobody. His brother is nobody. I'm nobody. They told me to get out of town and lie low, so that's what I'm doing."

"No, Laura. You're not nobody. I can't live with that."

God, he was gorgeous when he was bossy. She leaned in and kissed him for real, like she'd wanted to all night, like he was her air and she'd never get enough. Derek's hands moved from her arms to her neck and he pulled her closer for a second kiss, a third, a kiss meant to steal her soul and break her spirit, make her stay.

And when it was over, she pulled back far enough to break his hold and stood up. When he leaned forward to follow, she held up her hand, palm out, to stop him. "No, Derek. I will not bring my bullshit to your family table. You've got people to protect. A family. I'm nobody. I won't risk you or your brothers."

"You can't leave like this. I won't let you."

"What are you going to do, Derek? Tie me to the bed?" Oh, no. Why had she said that? Never mind. She knew why. Two reasons. One, to distract Derek. And two? Well, because the idea had entered her mind more than once the last few hours.

"If I have to."

It was a lie and they both knew it. She hadn't known him long, but he'd kept his word every step of the way. And he'd promised to hold her, and he'd promised to let her go. "You promised me. Last night you promised you'd let me go in the morning."

He was shaking his head, but she could see the resignation in his eyes, the internal battle. He'd given his word.

She ran her hand through her hair, realizing she'd been an idiot. "I'm sorry. I shouldn't have told you. I don't want my last memory of you to be a fight."

She had him. She'd won. She could see it in the way his shoulders slumped and his eyes darkened with pain. She hated to hurt him, but she'd hate for his family to get sucked into her mess even more. Maybe, in a few weeks, when the trial was over…

When it was over... She closed her eyes. She couldn't stay, but she couldn't bear the thought of never seeing him again either. "Give me your phone number. If everything works out..."

"You mean if you're not dead."

"...I'll call you in six weeks."

"What's in six weeks?"

"The trial."

"No."

"No?" She blinked in shock and tried to process what he was saying. "You don't want me to call you?"

"No. I won't wait six weeks. Don't tell me where you're going. Fine. Don't tell me your real name. Fine. But I want a text every damn day so I know you're all right. And so you can reach me if you need help." He got out of bed, moving fast, too fast for her to escape. "I'm a man of my word, Laura. I see the look in your eye. I know you think you're doing the right thing. Fine. I'll let you walk out of here, but that's my condition. Your number. And a message every day." He pulled her close, pressed her to his chest. He'd slept with his pants on, thank god, but the raw heat of his skin was like a brand.

She wrapped her arms around him and leaned up to kiss him on the jaw. It was nice, knowing someone would care if she disappeared, someone other than the prosecuting attorney in Benny's case. And she didn't want Derek to worry. "All right."

Squeezing him tightly, she walked back to the small

desk and wrote her number down on the writing pad. He hadn't seen her note yet, and she wanted to be gone before he did.

It was stupid, what she'd written. Stupid and whimsical and not at all like her. But there was no sneaking past him to take it off the pillow. She's written it thinking she'd never see him again. Now? Now she had to get out of here before he found it—and she couldn't bear to look him in the eye.

Holding out the piece of paper with her number on it, she sighed with relief when he took it from her and kissed her one more time.

"Goodbye, Derek."

He let her go, but his final words made her turn around as she opened the door.

"It's not goodbye, Laura. This is not goodbye."

She hoped she lived long enough to prove him right.

———

Denver

Sweat gathered in his hair and ran down the side of his face beneath the welding mask as he put the finishing touches on his latest creation, a Ducati Monster cut up and outfitted for off-road racing. The bike was a thing of monstrous beauty, powerful, and fast enough to feed the twisted need every adrenaline junkie had to cheat death. The client was going to pick it up in a few hours and Derek flamed the edges of the welds, making sure they were smooth and perfect. A work of fucking art.

"Yo, Derek. Line 2." His business manager, Connor, shouted over the crashing of metal banging on metal, drills, compressors and general sounds of an active garage. This was Derek's second home and he loved everything about it, the smell of gasoline, oil, grease and tires spread over concrete like frosting on a birthday cake. The back end, the shop, was where he felt the most alive. The front end, with its European bikes on display, leathers, gloves, and every other gadget and pretty thing his high-end clientele wanted on display in a renovated warehouse, made him cranky. He was damn good at what he did, but he preferred to be in the back, getting dirty. Not up front wowing clients with his custom portfolio. He preferred to let his work speak for itself.

Derek nodded that he'd heard and shut down his torch. Connor wouldn't bother him in the garage unless it was important.

Derek set his gear aside and turned off the supply line to his torch, making sure everything was all the way off before walking back inside to his tiny, cramped office. The room was really meant to be a supply closet, but it held a desk, a telephone, a chair and his drawing table where he spent hours giving life to his new custom creations on paper before bringing them into the real world.

Under his design book he kept another, this one filled with faces. His mom. His abuela. His brothers and their wives. Everyone who was important to him had been captured and analyzed, the smallest nuances of their expressions brought to life by the subtle shading of his pencil leads. And in the back of that book were clippings of tropical islands and jungle paradises he'd always wanted to see. In the military he'd been sent to sit on a base in Germany for two years. Beer and brats as exotic as he got over there. He'd gone to the Middle East after that, two years of sand and sweat and the nearly constant roar of helos taking off and landing. He'd been a mechanic, even then, and could fix just about anything that moved. Tracks or wheels.

But he couldn't fix Laura. Hell, he didn't even know where she was. True to her word, she'd sent him one message each day with an update. She was safe. She had a place to stay. She got a new job. But when he probed, or asked questions?

Silence. Well, not silence, exactly. She had a habit of sending him the most annoying GIFs on the planet in response to his questions. Some funny as hell, some seductive. But none of them real answers.

She liked to play, but he didn't want funny memes or half-answers. He wanted facts.

Screw that. He wanted her here, where he could keep his eye on her.

No one knew about his art. His stepfather had beat him for drawing when he was younger and his mother never cared. He'd learned a long time ago to hold tight to the things he loved, to protect them from prying eyes and angry fists.

He flipped through the pages to the newest drawing and traced the lines of her face with the tip of his index finger. Laura's face taunted him from the page. He'd drawn her sleeping, her full lips relaxed, her haunted expression hidden by closed eyes. He'd watched her for over an hour, soaking her in. He'd even taken a picture of her on his phone and kept it secret. She would have made him delete it, he was sure. He'd thought to delete the photo himself, but as many times as he chastised himself for being a sentimental fool, he could never press that little trashcan icon in the corner with his finger. Then she'd be gone. Really gone. Nothing but a figment of his imagination and a hastily scribbled note that he had clipped to the page.

He'd read it at least a thousand times. Every time his body became heavy with regret and determination burned through him.

He *would* find her. He *would* see her again. He had to.

And if he hadn't taken the picture, he wouldn't have the drawing. He'd used the photo as a base, but when he put pencil to paper the image leaped from the page, somehow more alive, more vibrant.

The second image of her he'd drawn from memory,

or perhaps fantasy. Her hair was mussed, her eyes dark, her lips swollen from his kisses. The image was burned into his mind like a brand.

How the hell had he become obsessed with a woman he'd only known for a few hours? A woman who wouldn't tell him her last name, or where she was? And why? To protect *him*. To protect his family. That was *his job*. Not hers. The irony of it all made him crazy and cost him hours of sleep.

Slamming the book closed, he shoved it back into his desk. "Damn stubborn woman."

"Hey man, you gonna grab that call or what?" Connor stuck his head in the tiny office and Derek nodded. Hell.

"Yeah. Sorry."

Connor nodded and took off, back to his big, shiny office with glass doors and windows. The large, showy office was all for Connor, along with all the foot traffic, mail, accounting and other day to day operations Derek didn't want to handle anymore.

Connor could keep the big desk, the glass door, fucking potted plants and all the headaches that came with it. The company had been growing steadily the last five years which was great for the bottom line, but an administrative headache that Derek had neither the patience nor the temperament to deal with. He built bikes. He didn't figure out the percentage of costs on a bid for parts, or haggle with suppliers. That was Connor's job.

But the shop, the back end, the grease and metal? That was Derek's realm and another problem entirely. It was December, and most of the hard-core bike mechanics he used and trusted in the summer months had headed south for the winter, chasing sunny skies and ocean breezes. Unfortunately, the shop was swamped, bikes backed up for weeks waiting to be worked on before spring returned to the Rockies.

If he didn't get a mechanic in here soon, he'd be working eighteen-hour days all over again, and he just didn't want to do that.

Hell, he was going to be thirty next month, but some days, after kneeling on the concrete for hours, or bent over working on an engine, he felt fifty years older.

Derek sat in his navy blue office chair and picked up the phone. The shop only had two lines, the first one was lit a solid green, the second flashing, waiting for him as he picked up the old-school, wired receiver and hit the button.

"This is Derek."

"Derek?" A small, scared voice came over the line and Derek's shoulders went ramrod straight.

"Brandon? Is that you? Are you okay, little man? What's going on?" Brandon O'Shea was twelve years old and in foster care. His mother was in and out of jail on prostitution and drug charges and his dad was in the state house for running meth up and down Highway 85 through all of northern Colorado. The kid had been through hell, and now Derek was his mentor through a local charity. He'd only known the kid for a few months, but what Derek claimed for his own, he protected. "Why didn't you call my cell?"

"You didn't answer."

Oh, hell. He'd been welding, and his cell phone was staring up at him with four missed calls right on top of his desk. "Sorry, buddy. What's up?"

"My mom's coming home next week. They want me to go talk to Murphy."

Oh, shit. Murphy was the judge who had been handling Brandon's case. Derek was all for reuniting children with their parents, if their parents had their shit together. Megan O'Shea did not. "It will be all right. The judge isn't stupid. He'll do the right thing."

"My mom is freaking out, and acting like everything's okay. It's not okay. I don't know what to do." Brandon's *mom*, Peggy Davis, was a fifty-seven year old foster mother who took care of six boys the best she could. It wasn't paradise, but compared to where most of the boys came from, it was damn close. "Mrs. Benson is going to be there, too. It's serious, Derek. I'm freaked."

"It'll be all right." Mrs. Benson was Brandon's social worker and held more sway over the decision than the rest. According to Brandon, she was an older woman and a complete hard ass that didn't take any shit off any of the kids she took care of. She'd let Brandon spend the night in a juvenile detention facility after he shoplifted for the fourth or fifth time. Maybe it worked, because

Brandon hadn't done it since, but Derek still thought she was a bitch for scaring the shit out of an eleven year old. Tough love, she'd told Brandon. Derek had wanted to bitch slap her into next week.

"Come with me."

Derek shook his head. He didn't have time, but he already knew there was no fucking way he could turn the kid down. There was an ocean of swallowed pride in the boy's request. "When?"

"In an hour. Two-thirty."

Derek sighed, making sure that Brandon didn't hear him. The kid didn't need to feel unwanted, or be handed a dose of guilt for asking for help. There wasn't a damn thing Derek could do except sit there and hold the kid's hand, so that's what he'd do. "I'll be there."

"Okay." The relief in Brandon's voice assured Derek he'd made the right decision as he hung up the phone. He pulled his black leather jacket down off the hook on the back of his door and grabbed his cell phone.

"Connor, I'm out."

"We got two bikes scheduled for pickup tomorrow," Conner replied.

"I know. I'll be in early. Hire a mechanic while I'm gone." Derek looked around the sparkling clean showroom housed in the antique brick building. The floor was a mix of shiny concrete and stripes painted red and black. The walls were lined with the latest custom gear, from leather to helmets and everything in between. And in the center of all the gadgets and gear, the bikes stood like fresh soldiers ready for war. Every time he looked at them, lined up and shining, he felt like he'd never seen anything so damn perfect.

"Already did, D. Started yesterday." Connor had the nerve to laugh at him. "George was back there with you all morning, man. Gonna work late tonight to get the order ready. Thought I'd let you know you don't have to come back in tonight."

"George?" *What?* He'd been so absorbed in what he was doing with the welds that he hadn't paid much attention to the far back corner of the garage. Yeah, he'd noticed someone moving around back there, but when he'd caught himself checking out the guy's ass, he'd made a point not to look in that direction for the rest of the day. Plenty of guys knew how to work on bikes, but a lot of them were either weekend warriors who had other jobs, or unreliable due to drugs, their nomadic lifestyle, or an independent streak that didn't adapt well to punching a time clock.

And he'd been in a black mood the last few days. The rest of the guys were avoiding him like the plague, which suited his current mood just fine. So, he hadn't looked too close, not interested in starting a conversation.

Connor nodded. "Yes. Goes by last name, George. Randolph George's kid."

"Holy shit. Seriously?" Derek craned his neck to get another view into the garage, but couldn't see anything through the small window in the swinging door. So, that tall, rounded ass he'd been checking out all morning, for unknown and somewhat disturbing reasons, belonged to Randolph George's son? The old man was a motorcycle stunt riding legend. Everyone in the world had heard of Evil Knievel, stunt man for the masses. But Randolph George was hard core. There wasn't an off-road racer alive who didn't know the name. Or hear about how he'd died. "And he knows what he's doing?"

Connor shrugged. "Fixed Billy Ferguson's bike in just a few hours yesterday."

Derek felt his eyes widen. Wow. That machine needed a complete overhaul of the engine and a new exhaust system.

"Yeah, right?" Connor grinned. "Admit it, D. I saved your ass. But George can only stay for about a month. I figured that would get us through Christmas and get us caught up, at least a little."

Yes, it would. Derek felt a small weight lift from his shoulders. With a wave he turned to leave as Connor kept talking to the two young men looking at Derek's portfolio on top of the glass display counter. The shop wasn't huge, but there were about thirty hardcore racing bikes lined up and sparkling like diamonds in the bright afternoon sunshine on the showroom floor. On the wall he had mounted five classic bikes he'd collected over the years and, on the lowest shelf where he could still get it down and race it once in a while, was his favorite Ducati, the fastest thing he'd ever had between his legs.

It was off-season now, winter in Colorado was not when most people were looking at motorcycles, and especially not the kind Derek created, off-road monsters, racing beasts, and any other crazy, custom shit his clients wanted. But the smart ones ordered now, because come April, the shop would be backed up with six or eight months of work. He had clients from all over the country, from Hollywood stars to professional racers. And he loved it, every minute, the challenge of making a bike do so much more than it had been engineered to do.

But as he started his Jeep, all he could think about was a scared little kid who really needed a big brother to sit next to him and hold his hand.

Wheels rolling, he glanced up to see his new mechanic walk out the side door of the shop, lift his head to the sky and take off his hat.

Dark hair fell like a curtain of silk halfway to hips that he could now clearly see were too curved to belong to any man. He slammed on the brakes and his tires squealed on pavement. At the sound, she turned to look at him, and his heart stopped as the one woman he couldn't stop thinking about, was convinced he'd never see again, blinked slowly, turned and stared right at him. Her face gave nothing away. It was as if the warm, vibrant woman he'd known in Las Vegas had given way to a statue of ice and glass.

7

"*L*aura." Her name a gut punch that stole all of his air.

He had been wondering what had happened to her, where she had gone and why. He had longed to feel her touch just one more time, to look deep into her eyes and get lost in them. He wanted to feel her silky smooth caramel colored skin, he'd have given anything-but yet here she was standing right in front of him like an apparition.

He blinked slowly and shook his head, afraid that once he opened his eyes again she would be gone, disappeared like smoke in the wind, a mere figment of his imagination. But there she was, still here, her beautiful curves in all the right places on perfect display, framed by the dusting of white snow on the ground behind her. She hadn't gotten any taller, and with work boots on instead of five-inch heels, she looked even smaller than he remembered.

She was dynamite in a small package. He wasn't fooled. But what was she doing here? Had she followed him after all? Had she played him in Vegas? Known the entire time who he really was? If she knew as much about motorcycles as it appeared, would it be a surprise that she'd known who he was the first time she'd seen him? He wasn't world famous, but he was well known in the business. Especially for someone as connected as Randolph George's daughter.

Slamming his Jeep into park, he opened the door and climbed out, momentarily forgetting where he had been racing to get so quickly. She had that kind of effect on him, a magnetic force he had trouble escaping.

His boots crunched on the sanded pavement as he approached her carefully, almost as if she were a fragile butterfly that would float away if he got too close to her.

"Laura?" Her name was a question, a desire, a heat bubbling up from within.

"Derek?" She stared at him dumbfounded, her dark eyes curious and full of an intensity he couldn't yet name. Having her next to him brought back all the feelings that had plagued him since that night in the Vegas hotel room.

Reaching for her, he pulled her close, hugging her because he couldn't fight the urge. The scent of wildflowers drifted up to him from her hair and he breathed deeply, filling his lungs with her as his body came back to life after what felt like a coma for the last few days.

"Do you work here?" she asked and that one question forced his brain back into gear, despite the fact that she was hugging him back. Thank fuck she was hugging him back.

"No. Do you?" He thought the question was stupid given that she was in an employee shirt and coveralls, but he asked it anyway because he was too shocked to say anything else. When she pulled away, he let her go, needing to see her face.

"Yep, you're looking at Walker Custom's newest mechanic." She stuffed her hands in her back pockets and winked at him while shrugging. "Are you looking for a bike? I can talk to Connor. As far as I can tell, he runs the place. I'm sure he'll get you a good deal."

Derek shook his head. Was this really possible? Did she truly not know who he was? "No. I definitely don't need another motorcycle."

She shrugged again, the movement a quick dart of her shoulders. "I'm not sure that's ever a rational response, but if you say so, I won't argue." He took a step closer, but now that the shock had worn off, she seemed better prepared and inched away from him.

"What are you doing here, Derek? Did you follow me?"

That stopped him in his tracks. "No. I was about to ask you the same question."

When her brows crinkled in confusion, he pointed to the sign hanging from the side of the building. "Walker Custom."

She glanced over her shoulder, read the sign and turned back to face him. "I know. I work here."

He held out his hand and stepped close. Lowering his voice, he tried not to stare at her lips, and failed. "Nice to meet you, Ms. George. I'm Derek Walker."

"Holy shit. You are not." Her eyes rounded in horror. "You're Derek Walker?"

"Since I was nine."

"What?" Her confusion irritated him, but not with her, with himself. Why was he bringing up his past? She didn't need to know his sad story, that he'd been adopted when he was nine and his name changed forever.

"Are you going to shake my hand or stare at me with your mouth open?"

"Oh, yes. Sorry." She placed her small hand in his and everything inside him shifted. She was here. He knew her name. This had to be fate, or God, or his mother helping him from the other side. His abuela had raised him Catholic, and even though he didn't go to mass, he remembered. And when she'd died? She had come to him in dreams for months, helping him cope, helping him survive. He didn't know if he believed in god or fate or random luck. She was standing in front of him. That was the only thing that mattered. "I can't believe it. I-I thought I'd never see you again."

"I guess it's fate."

"Fate?" She raised a cynical eyebrow. "No offense, Derek, but fate hasn't exactly been kind to me."

"Maybe it's trying to make amends." He leaned in, not able to control his instincts anymore. He had to kiss her, feel her lips, listen to the soft sound she made in the back of her throat when he touched her.

Shock and disappointment made him heavy as she used her hand to push his chest away.

"What's wrong?"

"Derek," she sighed, looked at the ground. "What we had in Vegas was great, special even. The connection was amazing."

"But," Derek said, having a feeling and a hunch about where this was going.

"*But,* that was Vegas. What happens in Vegas stays in Vegas. Nothing has changed for me."

"What does that mean?" He hated the resolve he saw in her eyes. He knew that look well, saw it in the mirror often enough. Laura was a woman used to doing what needed to be done.

"We can be friends. That's all. At least for now."

"Until the trial." The knife twisted in his heart but he couldn't argue, not here, not now. He had to be in court for Brandon and he was already running late.

"Yes. In fact, I shouldn't even be here. I should go. I'll let Connor know and find another job."

"Go where? Why?"

"Because this was supposed to be an anonymous

job. But I know you. You know who I am and why I'm here. Working for strangers was fine. But you? No, Derek. No. I don't want to put your family at risk in case psycho Benny's brother tracks me down. You have family to protect."

Protect his family. Protect his brothers at all costs. It had been his life's mission, his only reason for existing for almost as long as he could remember. She was right. He knew she was right. And it didn't matter.

"You're not going anywhere." The words came out harsher than he intended, but damn it, she was fucking with his head. She was practically a stranger, but that didn't matter. She was alone in the world, on the run and she needed him.

Hands on her hips now, she assessed him with those warm eyes, looking right through him. And he let her look, let everything show.

"Caveman much, Derek? I don't take orders very well, in case you were wondering."

"I wasn't." Taking a more subtle approach to his wild woman, he reached for her hand, relieved when she let him touch her. "There's no reason for you to go anywhere. No one else knows about the trial or why you're here. No one will talk, and you won't have to be alone." The last bit was a low, low blow. He knew it, but he wasn't beyond all out manipulation to convince her to stay. She needed help, that much was obvious. Combined with the fact that he hadn't been able to stop thinking about her, worrying about her, for days, and he would say whatever he had to say to keep her close.

"I'm used to taking care of myself, Derek."

He squeezed her hand. "I know. But it won't hurt to stick around here. I'm here. My brothers are here. You'll have friends around. And I need the help. I've got weeks of work stacked up in the garage." He wanted to be more than just her friend, but the light in her eyes wasn't mischief or happiness, it was determination, grit, an instinct for survival he recognized all too well. She was stubborn as hell. She'd proven that when she walked out of that Vegas hotel room. There would be no forcing her. She had to choose to stay.

"Look, I have to go. I need to be somewhere right now," Derek said, not wanting to go into detail. He gestured to his jeep, which was still running. "Can we talk when I get back?"

Laura bit her lip. If she said no, he'd have to wait to leave. He couldn't drive away if she was going to run. If the last few days had taught him anything, it was that he might never stop thinking about Laura George, even if he never saw her again. Somehow, she'd gotten under his skin.

When she shrugged, he let out the breath he'd been holding. "All right. Sure. Connor asked me to work late. Two clients want to pick up their bikes tomorrow and I could use the extra hours."

"Promise me, Laura. Promise me you'll be here when I get back."

She took far too long deciding, but he knew her well enough to know if she gave him her word, she'd keep it. "Okay. I'll be here. I promise."

"We'll talk when I get back." He ran to his jeep and peeled out of the parking lot. He was going to be late. Brandon was going to be freaked, and he hated breaking his word almost as much as he hated the thought of Laura disappearing on him again.

8

*L*aura

"Hey, George. I'm taking off. Want me to lock up?" Connor walked into the garage where Laura was polishing her wrenches for the fourth or fifth time. She was done. She'd been done for over an hour, but she'd made a promise to Derek and she meant to keep it.

"No thanks. I'm supposed to meet Derek here when he gets back."

Connor raised a brow but didn't say anything weird. Thank goodness. "Okay. I'm going to lock the front door. Everything else is locked up. You can get out, but no one can get in without a key."

"Great, thanks."

Connor watched her for a long, silent minute. "You

can wait in his office if you want. At least there's a chair in there. And it's not so damn cold."

That made her laugh. She'd been shivering, she knew it, but it was fifteen freaking degrees outside and she had desert blood. She'd spent most of her life in southern California and this biting cold was as foreign to her as the five inches of snow that dusted the ground outside.

"Okay. Thanks Connor." He nodded and patted the doorframe in farewell as he headed back out to the front of the shop. She set the wrench down and tossed the cleaning towel aside. "And you aren't getting any cleaner."

With a sigh of impatience she followed Connor out to the front and made her way to Derek's office. She'd never been in the small space before.

It felt like intruding. Like she was on sacred ground. But it was much warmer than the garage and she was not enough of a masochist to sit out there in the cold.

Maybe she should wait in Connor's office instead. It was bigger, with lots of windows and multiple chairs… and it didn't feel so *personal*.

She got up and walked across the showroom to the closed glass door.

Locked.

"Damn it." It was either sit at Derek's desk or wait out there in the cold. And that was not really an option now that she'd felt the heat coming off the electric baseboard along the wall behind Derek's desk.

Sitting down in his padded blue chair, she let her gaze wander, fascinated to be in such an intimate space. *His* space.

His desk was barren except for a computer monitor, mouse, keyboard, a pad of unused sticky notes and a desk set full of pencils. No pens. No stapler. No calculator. No clutter. Pencils. Mechanical. Yellow #2. Drafting pencils. Fat ones. Thin ones.

"You are a strange man, Derek Walker." She whispered the thought aloud and studied the calendar affixed to the wall directly in front of her. There he'd meticulously penciled in orders and due dates for various clients. Behind her the wall was covered with photographs of custom bikes he'd built himself, his signature in the bottom of each picture. Derek was in each photograph, standing next to the motorcycle with the machine's new owner. It was like that wall of diplomas always on display in a doctor's office, except Derek's credentials were beautiful, powerful machines instead of a degree from Harvard.

Looking at them, at the pride in his stance, the satisfaction in his eyes, she wanted to kiss him. He'd come up on his own, worked his ass off, and made something of himself. "Something sexy."

Just saying.

Next to the desk was a single, two-drawer file cabinet. The drawer was half closed, stuck on a hard black book of some kind. Sticking out of the book were a handful of pages that looked like they'd been pulled from the pages of a travel magazine filled with beach towels and palm trees.

Truly curious now, Laura pulled the book free and set it on the desk.

It was a sketchpad, black hardcover, with frayed corners and a well-worn spine. The paper inside was standard size, like opening a notebook without the spiral. Or the lines.

Feeling naughty, but unable to resist, Laura opened the book to a marked page and froze at the face staring up at her.

Her face.

Shaking, she traced the delicate line of her cheek with her index finger. "I don't look like this, Derek." She didn't. The drawing made her look soft and feminine, vulnerable and sexy, like a mythical siren, too beautiful to be real.

Shocked, she turned several pages and found more. All of his brothers were in there. She recognized them from the wedding. There were several drawings of an older woman with kind eyes. She would have had no clue who she was except Derek had written the word *Mom* in the corner. There were drawings of several motorcycles, a few animals, an eagle and a mountain lion. His brothers' new wives. Everyone important to him.

The last page was a second drawing of her, awake and staring up from the page like a siren, a come-hither look in her eyes and her lips swollen as if she'd just been kissed. Clipped to the drawing was the note she'd left him in the hotel.

You are amazing. Forget about me and find someone to love you. ~L

Tears came at her out of nowhere, all the feelings from that night rushing at her like an out of control train careening off the tracks.

She'd seen it happen on set. Her dad had been out there, dodging rolling train cars and jumping fiery debris. The whole thing had taken months to plan and lasted less than a minute. But the movie had been a blockbuster and that job had meant another win for her dad, another job…another move. Another school. More lonely hours in a trailer while her dad partied and played and did what he could to drown her mother's memory in whiskey.

Watching that movie scene had felt like this. Dangerous. Nerve-wracking and totally out of control. Like she was now. Like wanting something with Derek would be.

She pulled the magazine pages out of the back for sheer distraction. Glossy images of island paradises enticed her. Hawaii. Key West. French Polynesia. An island in Greece. There were at least a dozen. All sandy beaches, striped umbrellas and cool drinks. Paradise.

It wouldn't be hard to imagine lounging on one of those beach chairs with him next to her or rubbing suntan lotion on her back.

A loud bang followed by the slam of the front door

and Laura shoved everything back into place and put the sketchbook back in the drawer. All the way this time. There was a space for it, right at the front.

So organized, her Derek.

Who was she kidding? Derek wasn't *her* anything.

Derek stomped the snow off his shoes on the rug near the front door and Laura rose to meet him, leaning against the doorframe. "Hey."

He froze and looked up at her. "Hey. I was afraid you wouldn't be here."

"I gave you my word."

"I know." He swiped his feet one last time and walked toward her. "But that took a helluva lot longer than I wanted it to. And there was an accident on I-25. Took me two hours to get back here."

"Where were you?" She shouldn't ask. She had no right to ask.

"I mentor a kid downtown. He had to go to court because his drug addict mother is getting out of jail and she wants him back. Well, she doesn't want him, she wants the money the state will give her to take care of him. Poor kid is scared to death."

"How old is he?"

"Twelve."

Crossing her arms, she studied him. "You are a saint among men, Derek Walker."

He frowned. "I'm no saint, Laura." He closed the distance until he was right in front of her, breathing her air. "I'm just a guy who knows what it's like on his side of that equation."

What? What was he talking about? "I don't understand. You and your brothers? You have an amazing family."

Lifting a hand, he grabbed a strand of her hair and rubbed it between his fingers. "We all came from hell-holes, Laura. My mom was an addict who overdosed when I was young. My dad drank himself to death, and beat me whenever he missed her too much. My abuela was the only person in the world who loved me and when she died it was all I could do to survive until I was adopted. Mitchell. Chance. Jake. We all survived hell. We were all adopted by our mother. Once we were brothers, I made sure we stayed together, watched each other's backs. No one messed with us after that. No one."

"Or what?" Holy crap. Mitchell was a surgeon. Chance was a lawyer. Jake ran a ranch that she'd been told was worth a fortune. And Walker Custom? Derek had to be a millionaire in his own right. She'd been teasing Derek at the wedding about beating up the other kids on the playground, but what he was saying took it to a whole new level. How had four boys with the world against them made it?

"I made sure they didn't do it again."

And there was her answer. Determination. Resolve. The man in front of her made it happen, that's how. "And if your brothers stepped out of line?"

"Same."

That made her chuckle. "That's what I thought." She wrapped her arms around herself and took a step back toward the heater. "You wouldn't have been able to keep me in line, I'm afraid."

When he raised a brow at her challenge she burst out laughing. "I had half a dozen fathers on set at any given time. And when my dad wasn't working, we were hanging around motorcycle clubs. I doubt you could do what six grown men couldn't."

"Try me."

9

———

*L*aura was laughing now, but he'd seen it, the fleeting pity that she quickly tried to hide. Now why the hell had he brought all that up? His parents? The beatings? All the shit he'd gone through as a kid? Not to make her feel sorry for him, that was for damn sure.

Pity was the last thing he wanted to see in her eyes. Mad lust? Laughter? Anything but pity. Time for a change of subject. "So, when is the trial?"

Mention of her troubles drained the laughter right out of her. "January 7th."

"And you have to be back in Vegas to testify?"

"Yes."

"And you'll stay here until then? So I can keep an eye on you?"

"No." She crossed her arms again and it was irritation that shined from her eyes now. Challenge. All it did was make him want to kiss her. God, she was gorgeous when she was all riled up and giving him sass. "I'm staying because you need a mechanic and I need a job."

The question was a mistake he couldn't stop himself from making. "Is that the only reason?"

Her sass turned to sadness, and he didn't like that look any more than he liked the pity. "Until January 7th, yes. That's the only reason, Derek. We can be friends, but that's all."

"What if I want more?"

"Then you're crazy."

"What if I'm crazy?"

She shook her head but stepped forward and hugged him, hard and fast. Before he could react, she'd let him go and was heading for the front door. "Then I'll just have to save you from yourself."

The door closed behind her with a slam and he grinned. How many times had he said the exact same thing to his brothers? But in those instances, he'd been right. This time...he was still right. Laura was going to be more than just his friend, but if she was scared and freaked out about the trial, then he'd wait to push her. He could afford to be patient now that he knew she was safe.

And he needed details.

Pulling out his cell phone he called his brother, the lawyer. If anyone could dig through the mess of the Nevada state court system and figure out what was going on, it was his baby brother. Chance answered on the second ring.

"Hey, Derek. What's up?" The loud banging of drums and guitar riffs filtered through the background and Derek cringed. Erin and her crew must be having a jam session in the basement again. Either that, or they were over at the Castillo house making the neighbors suicidal.

"How the hell can you stand all that noise?"

Chance laughed and blared a guitar note into the phone. "We're practicing. The band is being extra quiet just for you." A cymbal crashed in the background and Derek chuckled. Extra quiet. Right. "What do you need?"

"I need your help, lawman."

———

LAURA, CHRISTMAS EVE

KNEELING ON THE COLD CONCRETE FLOOR, LAURA tightened the last bolt on a new exhaust system install and smiled. She was alone in the shop, working, killing time rather than sitting home feeling sorry for herself for being all alone on Christmas Eve. Well, she was used to being alone. What she was *not* used to was *missing Derek.* She'd spent years alone. She'd gone to nine high schools and lived all over the world.

Wherever her dad went, he took her along. Her only real friend had been her motorcycle and the open road. Until Derek, that had been enough. Now she wasn't just alone, she was lonely, and that made her grumpy at Christmas.

Not that she'd had time to do much moping around lately. No. Her life had exploded. She had so much going on, she didn't know how she coped. Well, she did, but she just had difficulty believing this was her life most of the time.

She'd known Derek for two weeks now. Met his family. Watched him laugh and smile and scowl. Watched him take the good-natured ribbing from all three of his brothers and their wives. They were a tight group and she always felt like an intruder, like the starving orphan with her nose pressed to the glass window—from the outside.

"Enough already." She scolded herself and went to put her tools away.

A local Denver radio station played Christmas music 24/7 and she had it cranked up to high volume. Yesterday, she'd gone online and bought Derek's gift. It was crazy. A bit too much. But since she'd seen the pictures in Derek's office, she couldn't stop thinking about it. And because impulse control wasn't normally high on her to-do list, she'd shelled out the cash with a huge grin and a spring in her step.

She owed him so much more than this one, small thing. Right?

God, he was going to *freak.*

Every day she worked with Derek and the other guys in the shop. Connor had become a fast friend. She loved what she was doing and didn't have to look over her shoulder every moment of every day. Derek told Connor not to report her to the state's employment department until after the trial, so there was no official record of her being here. No electronic trail. She paid for everything with cash...when Derek let her pay for anything at all.

Much to her disappointment, he'd been the perfect gentleman, played the part of a friend and nothing more. If he went out for lunch, he brought back food for the whole crew. And every night, he drove her home or took her to one of his brother's homes for dinner. She'd spent time with Mitchell and Jessica and oohed and aahed over new baby Tommy's room. He was due in just a few weeks and the entire family was on pins and needles. Mitchell, the doctor, was hilarious. He constantly spoke to his son as if the little one could understand him already, giving him advice and making him promises.

Jake and Claire had come into town twice from their mountain home and Laura had heard all about Claire's awesome trip to Italy and her archeological dig at Herculaneum—a town near Pompeii that Laura never knew existed—and how exciting it was to uncover new artifacts. Claire practically glowed, and Derek's brother, Jake, rarely let her out of his sight. Apparently, she'd been gone for several months and he was making up for lost time. Laura had walked into the kitchen for a glass of water and turned around as fast as her little feet could take her.

Jake and Claire had been…occupied, and didn't notice she was there. She'd laughed, grabbed Derek by the hand and pulled him out of the house. He's sputtered a question until he heard something hit the floor in the kitchen followed by Claire's squeals of laughter. After that, they'd bolted, spending a solid hour at a local ice cream shop to give Jake and Claire time to…finish whatever they were doing in Derek's tiny kitchen.

Last but not least, they'd spent time with the youngest Walker brother. Chance and Erin were wild, and fun, and Erin was a rock star. And Jessica's family were rock stars. Literally. Freaking rock stars. The Band Castillo was world famous and three days ago, Laura sat at a dinner table and laughed until she cried as Jessica's sweet neighbor, an elderly black woman named Miss Bea – who was ninety if she was a day – ran the whole show. Chance and Erin had come over, the musicians had started messing around, making up songs with lyrics so crazy no one could ever sing them with a straight face. But then Miss Bea brought out chocolate-caramel-toffee crunch muffins and everything else had been forgotten.

She was smiling when Derek walked into the garage wearing jeans and a black t-shirt. That was pretty much all he ever wore, which was just fine with her. With his black hair and dark eyes, he looked like a sex god.

"What are you smiling about?" he asked.

"I was just remembering the lyrics to *Crazy Monkey Rex* and Miss Bea's muffins."

His smile made her heart skip a beat. He'd been doing it a lot lately. Smiling. And Claire had pulled her aside a couple days ago to make sure Laura knew that was not part of Derek's normal behavior pattern. In fact, the Walker wives were scheming already, planning Laura's wedding. It was kind of cute, but mostly it just made her sad.

They were so far from that kind of relationship, forever sounded impossible.

"You want to get out of here? I could use your help." Derek looked unsure, and that wasn't like him at all.

Tossing her work aside, she walked to the sink and washed up. "Sure. What do you need help with?"

"Women."

"What?" She about dropped the towel she was using to dry her hands.

"My new sisters. Miss Bea. Jessica's sister, Sophia. This is the first year they're all part of the family for Christmas and I have absolutely no idea what to get them."

Ahhhh. The relief she felt was about ten times stronger than it should have been, but she wasn't going to examine it too closely. "Shopping is fun. And I need to get a few things myself. How long do we have?"

Derek checked his phone. "The mall stays open until midnight tonight. So, we have about seven hours to make sure I don't look like an ass on Christmas morning."

Laughing, she grabbed her coat. "Then let's go. But I have one condition."

He sighed. "You and your conditions, woman. What is it this time?"

"You and me. We're getting a picture with Santa."

He studied her for several seconds as she bounced up and down on her toes. Hell yeah, she was serious. She'd been all over the world, but her dad didn't make time for stuff like that. "Look, Derek, my dad hated standing in line almost as much as he hated shopping. Which meant all the years I was growing up there were no malls, no Christmas shopping, and no…"

"Santa."

"Exactly." She had gifts every year. And they'd always been invited over to someone else's home for Christmas dinner. She hadn't *not* had Christmas, it just hadn't been *hers*.

"All right. Santa it is. Let's go."

"Yes!" She pumped her fist and winked at him as he held the door open for her with a grin.

"You're crazy. You know that?"

"I thought you said you were the crazy one."

"Maybe we're both crazy."

She smiled so hard her cheeks hurt. "Maybe we are."

When they got to the mall, it was packed with shoppers, parents taking their kids to see Santa and other people wandering around looking in store windows just to admire the decorations and soak in the cheery atmosphere.

They had ridden in Derek's jeep. Laura was dressed head to toe in jeans, boots, a scarf that covered her face, gloves and a hat. The weather here was certainly something to get used to after coming from the desert of Las Vegas. She enjoyed the coziness of the freshly fallen snow though, it made the holidays pop even more in her mind. She would get a white Christmas for the first time in her life and she couldn't wait to wake up on Christmas morning to a blanket of white with beautiful icicles shimmering in the sunlight.

They raced as carefully as they could across the parking lot, wanting to get inside and away from the bitter cold that took their breath away. Laura dodged a few patches of ice, but skid across more on her flat-bottomed boots.

Derek was holding the door for her, looking at her with a look she'd seen a lot of lately. She wasn't sure if he found her amusing or idiotic in her adventures. But she'd always been the kind of girl to stomp the mud puddles whether she was wearing a rain slicker and plastic boots or a Sunday dress and pretty sandals.

Picking up a handful of snow, she packed it into a ball and threw it at Derek. She shouted in victory as it exploded on the arm of his coat, puffing out into a burst of fun.

"Hey! What was that for?" Derek grinned at her as she walked past him, but he wasn't done with her. He grabbed her from behind and tickled her until she squealed in protest. "Don't tempt me again, Laura. I have a hard enough time keeping my hands off you."

"Then don't."

"Tease." His eyes darkened as he tickled her again, making her shriek with delight. A family passing through looked at them like they were crazy but she didn't care. She was bound and determined to have some fun today.

When they got inside her mouth immediately dropped. There was Christmas music playing over the loud speakers giving the entire place a cozy, feel-good quality. A giant tree, lit up and decorated with ribbons, bows and ornaments, dazzling and enormous, it rose to touch the ceiling of the two-story entrance. It must have been twenty feet tall. "Wow."

Derek took her by the hand, their fingers entwined. "Shop now, look later. We're on the clock."

"Okay." She let Derek drag her past the huge tree, until she saw what was hidden in the base along the opposite side. "Derek! Come on! Hurry! They close in thirty minutes." She was the one pulling him along now, to the back of the line. Santa's helpers looked them over with raised brows, but Laura stared at the teenaged girls in elf suites with the evil eye. This was sooo happening. Tugging on Derek's arm, she squeezed his hand and leaned into his side. "What are you going to ask for?"

"What?" He looked down at her, surprise in his eyes.

"Well, you can't just sit on his lap and not ask for something."

"I am *not* sitting on Santa's lap, Laura. That is not happening."

10

She rolled her eyes but knew she wasn't going to win this one. He was playing along, but she could only push him so far. "All right. Fine. But I am, and you have to stand right next to me in the picture."

He was silent for a few minutes as a brother and sister climbed onto Santa's lap in front of them. The bigger girl had pigtails and a delighted smile. She looked like she was about five. Her little brother was fighting back tears at the big, scary old man holding him. He was about two years old and so adorable she wanted to go squeeze him.

Smiling until her cheeks ached, she realized she hadn't been this happy in months. Maybe years…since the murder six months ago, since her father's death before that.

There were tinsel, garland and nutcracker

decorations splashed throughout almost every square inch of the mall. There were people everywhere, dressed in red, green and other holiday type outfits. A joyous elf passed them and waved, completely decked out in an adorable green suit with a green hat and a bell at the bottom.

Laura waved back animatedly. She looked at Derek who smiled at her, but she could tell he was not as into all this festive stuff as she was, which made the moment that much more special. He was doing this for her.

When the little ones scrambled off Santa's lap, she hurried up and perched on his knee. He was a fabulous Santa, a truly elderly gentleman with a real white beard and gentle, sparkling blue eyes. She tugged Derek along and pulled him to the side, determined to have him in her photograph.

"Well, young lady. What do want to ask Santa for this Christmas?" The old man smiled at her and she sighed in relief. He didn't think she was crazy or a complete weirdo for being here. Even better, he seemed genuinely kind.

She kissed him on the cheek, because she could, and leaned over to whisper in his ear.

Tears threatened, but he just smiled when she pulled away and nodded in complete understanding. "I'll see what I can do."

"Thank you, Santa." She grinned and lifted her head as one of Santa's elves told her to smile and look into the camera. When it was over, she shooed Derek away and bought two copies, one for herself and one for Derek. Each in a cheery Christmas frame.

They were ridiculously expensive, but she didn't care. This was truly once in a lifetime. She paid for the digital file too, and gleefully typed in her email so she could download the photo to her phone later.

Derek waited for her, his shoulder leaning against a pillar decorated with sparkling red ribbon. "You ready?"

"Yep." She reached for his hand. "Let's do this."

They made quick work of the night, finding something for each one of the new women in Derek's family and something for each of his brothers as well. They sipped hot cocoa and laughed at the frantic expressions they saw on numerous men who had apparently left their shopping to the last minute on Christmas Eve.

"What is it with men and last minute shopping?"

They both caught site of a frazzled looking man wearing worn out tennis shoes, high-water pants and a shirt that looked like it had been on the receiving end of a toddler's spaghetti dinner. His hair was sticking up oddly and he had dark circles under his eyes. He was pushing a stroller that held sleeping twins who looked about a year old. Laura nodded her chin to him and laughed. "Poor guy. He looks frazzled."

Derek studied the man for a moment. "Yeah, but he looks happy."

Laura looked closer. "How can you tell?" Fascinated

by Derek's odd response, she held her breath waiting to see what he would say.

"It's in his eyes, in the way he looks at his kids."

Studying the man, she focused all of her attention on the young dad's face. Derek was right. Whenever he looked at the sleeping babies his gaze softened with a look Laura had seen from her own dad a handful of times. More often she'd seen it in movies, read about it in books. Love. It was love.

Clearing her throat, she stood. "Well, it's getting late. We should probably go."

"All right. I'll drive you home."

She shook her head. "No. I need my car. Just take me back to the shop."

They made their way to his frost-coated Jeep and she huddled inside with the heater blasting cold air as Derek scraped off the windows. They drove to the shop in silence with Christmas music playing softly on the radio. When he pulled into the parking lot, she couldn't take it anymore.

"Wait here. I have something for you."

"For me?" he asked.

"Just wait here." She hurried to the beater car she'd bought off a used car lot and opened the creaky door. She really needed to oil that.

She'd wrapped the envelope in a small box so he wouldn't be able to guess what it was. It looked like a rectangular box of chocolates wrapped in silver and gold with an oversized ribbon. Feeling awkward now, thinking this may have been the single most idiotic thing she'd ever done on impulse—and that was saying something—she opened the passenger door and handed him the gift. "You can't open this until tomorrow."

He was shaking his head. "No, Laura. You didn't need to get me anything."

"Just shut-up and take it, Derek." Tucking a strand of hair behind her ear, she looked him in the eye and sighed. "I…you…look, you've been so amazing since I met you. First Vegas and then letting me work here. I wanted to do something special for you." She knew she was blushing, but couldn't control the heat rising to her cheeks. Hopefully, he'd just think it was the cold. "But you can't open it until tomorrow. Okay?"

"All right."

"Promise me."

That made him grin. "I promise."

"Good." Smiling in relief, she stepped back, her hand on the door. "I'll see you in a couple days."

"What?"

"After Christmas. The shop is closed tomorrow, right?"

Scowling at her, he shook his head. "No. I'll pick you up at your place at nine. We're going over to Mitchell's house for Christmas. Everyone is going. The Castillos will be there, and Miss Bea. Jessica's dad said he might fly in, which should be interesting since she refers to him as 'the sperm donor', but with a grandson on the way, I think he wants to mend fences with his kids."

"So, you're inviting me to a family soap opera for Christmas?"

"You think I want to face all that drama alone?"

That made her laugh. "All right. I'll see you at nine."

She closed the door and walked to her car. Thankfully, it started and Derek hopped out of his Jeep to scrape off her windows. He was always doing things like that, little things, things that made her feel special.

On impulse, she kissed him on the cheek as he held her car door open. "Thanks for a great night."

"My pleasure."

She buckled in but he hadn't closed the door. "I'll follow you home. The roads are slick and your tires are shit."

"Okay." The offer was appreciated. The tires on this used beater had very little tread left and the roads were slicked with partially melted snow that had turned smooth as glass when the sun set and the temperature dropped. "Thanks."

He closed her door and got in his car to follow behind her. It was only a couple miles to her worn-down studio apartment, but she didn't want to slide off the road and have to walk home in the dark. Alone.

She was halfway home when bright headlights came out of nowhere.

She didn't hear the giant truck until it slammed into

the driver's door. All she heard was the roar of the truck's engine, the crash of metal and her own screams.

————

THE CRICK IN HIS NECK MADE HIM SHIFT IN THE STIFF CHAIR next to Laura's hospital bed. Her small hand was in his, his only connection to her. He wanted to climb into that bed and hold her.

Who was he kidding? He wanted to crawl inside her skin, get so close she'd never be able to leave him again. He needed her close so he could protect her. Keep her safe. Touch her. Kiss her. Smell her. See her smile.

She was still unconscious, the stitches on the side of her forehead covered in white gauze and tape. Her left cheek was bruised a terrible mash of purple and black and the pain meds the docs gave her had knocked her out.

Derek's insides churned like he'd swallowed a blender filled with acid. He hadn't felt this helpless since his abuela died and all he could do was hold her hand until the fragile old woman, the only person in the world he loved at the time, and the only person in his young life who loved him back, stopped breathing. They'd dragged him away kicking and screaming, fighting to stay with her.

He felt like that now. Desperate. A little lost. How this woman could mean so much to him after such a short time, he didn't know, didn't understand, but when that jacked-up truck came out of nowhere and T-boned Laura's car, his world went on tilt and hadn't recovered.

Mitchell opened the door and peaked around the corner.

Thank god.

Waiting for someone to tell him what the fuck was going on was driving him crazy. He'd followed the ambulance in, lied to the hospital staff and said he was her fiancé. They'd let him sit with her, but no one had told him anything. She was out cold and all the scans, MRI's and other bullshit they did in hospitals? He hadn't heard a damn thing.

Normally, his first impulse would be to stand and greet his brother, but that would mean letting go of Laura's hand and he couldn't do that. Somehow he was convinced she could feel him, know that she wasn't alone.

"What's wrong with her?" he asked. He didn't have time for bullshit and Mitchell had come down even though it was his night off. He wore his white doctor's coat and had a stethoscope around his neck. He carried a clipboard with paperwork piled almost half an inch thick.

Mitchell lifted a hand to placate him. "She's going to be fine, Derek."

"Tell me everything. These nurses won't talk."

"They didn't have the results back. The techs can't read tests or give results. You know the rules."

"Just tell me."

Mitchell looked down, shuffling through the reports. "Her blood work is normal. She's got a mild concussion. The bruising on her cheek will hurt for a few days, but she didn't fracture any bones, which is lucky. The single laceration took twenty-three stiches, but that will heal in a couple weeks as well. Her internal organs are fine. She'll be sore for a few days, but she'll be fine."

Derek nodded as relief flooded him. Fuck this. She was staying at his place from now on. He wasn't letting her out of his sight. He studied her face, the soft curve of her lips, remembered the bright look in her eyes when she'd been sitting on Santa's lap, her joy at seeing all the Christmas decorations, how she smiled at everyone who walked by and talked to every single person under the age of four. She was so full of life. Seeing her like this was breaking something inside him, something he'd patched up with super-glue and duct tape when he'd become a Walker, when he'd been given a new chance with a new family.

She was destroying him, breaking him open, and it hurt.

Mitchell walked to the opposite side of her bed. "What about the hit and run? What did the police say?"

Ice cold fury rolled through him and he stroked his thumb gently over the back of her hand. "There were no video cameras. The truck was black and the windows were tinted. No license plate. The steel grill on the front cut through her car like a hammer through aluminum foil."

"So, they've got nothing."

"Nothing. But I know who did it. She knows."

"What are you talking about?" Mitchell's tone went dark. "Derek, I love you brother, but what the fuck is going on with you two? I know it was random chance that we ran into her in Vegas. But then she shows up here, working for you. And you bring her around like she's yours, but you both tell everyone you're just friends. And now this? Are you saying this wasn't an accident?"

11

———

"It wasn't an accident. And I've been waiting for the time to be right, trying to be patient, trying to be a damn gentleman." It was time to make a few calls. The first to his brother Chance to find out what he'd been able to learn about Laura's murder trial. "She's hiding out in Denver waiting to testify in a murder trial."

"What?"

Derek stared at her, at the blood on the edges of her bandage, at the bruise on her beautiful face. "I thought she'd be safe. We didn't know they found her." Lowering his head to the mattress, he pulled air into his lungs. In. Out. He wanted to kill someone, but he didn't have a target, a name, anything.

"Who?"

"I don't know."

Mitchell sat down in a chair across from him and

repeated some advice Derek had given him not too long ago. "Maybe it's time to walk away, Derek."

The irony was not lost on him when he gave his brother the same response Mitchell had given him about his wife, Jessica. "I don't think I can."

Silence. Derek lifted his head to see Mitchell studying Laura before looking back at him. "So, she's family now?"

"If she'll have me."

"Fucking A, big brother. It's about damn time." Mitchell grinned, but the humor in his eyes faded as he looked down at the medical records in his hands once more. "She's stable. She doesn't need to be in here as long as she's not going home alone."

That made Derek almost violent. "She's not going anywhere alone."

Mitchell's grin was back. "That's what I thought you'd say. We need to get her out of here before whoever was in that truck figures out she's still alive and comes back for round two."

"I agree." Derek lifted her hand to his lips and kissed her, careful of the IV just above her wrist. "Where can we go? I don't think she'll be safe at my apartment either."

Mitchell took out his phone and dialed. It was 2:30 AM, but this was family. Derek heard a deep, rumbling voice on the other end before Mitchell spoke. "Hey, Jake. We have a situation."

The ranch. Perfect. It was big, out of the city, and

Jake and Claire had adopted three very protective German Shepherd pups from a rescue a few months ago. And if someone came at Laura again?

The ranch was stocked with rifles and lots of places to bury a dead body. He knew how to kill, had done it overseas. It left a bitter taste in his mouth, but he'd do it to save Laura—without hesitation.

It was crazy thinking, but Derek didn't argue with the protective monster fighting its way out of him. If some murderous bastard came after Laura again, he'd do what he needed to do and fuck the consequences. He protected the people he loved. That's what he did. And for better or worse, he realized that list now included the woman lying hurt and alone in that sterile hospital bed.

Mitchell walked into the hallway speaking on the phone for a few minutes. When he was done, he came back in and locked the door. "It's set. Jake will be here in an hour with his truck. Only a suicidal idiot would try to ram you in that tank."

"That's not good enough."

"Agreed. Which is why I called Jessica. She called her sister, Sophia. Sophia's going to come down and change clothes with Laura. With her long dark hair, it'll look like Laura's still in the bed until morning. Laura can wear Sophia's clothes and put on a hat. I told Jake to pull up at the employee entrance near the cafeteria and we'll sneak her out that way. That will give you a few hours head start. Once you're out of the city, they'll have a hell of a time finding you. And your Jeep will still be in the lot. Give me your keys and I'll have Jake or Chance drive it to your place tomorrow."

It seemed extreme, like spy movie shit, but Derek agreed to all of it. Anything to keep Laura safe. If the police weren't going to protect her, the Walker brothers would. Now that he'd claimed her for his own, the whole family would close ranks. And he was never so grateful for his brothers.

"Thanks. I owe you one."

That made Mitchell laugh. "Are you kidding me with that shit, Derek? It's about damn time you needed some help. You've saved all of our asses more than once. So if she matters, if she's yours then she's ours now, too. So just shut the fuck up and let us do this."

———

THE LAST FEW HOURS WERE A BLUR. SHE KNEW DEREK, Mitchell and Sophia Castillo had been in her hospital room. She knew Derek helped her change her clothes, and then for some bizarre reason, Sophia put on a pair of pajamas and crawled into Laura's hospital bed. Mitchell hooked up all the electronic monitoring crap to his sister-in-law and Sophia laid down and closed her eyes like she was just taking a nap.

Mitchell put a hat on her head and wheeled her through what felt like a hundred miles of empty, out of the way corridors deep inside the hospital.

They came out into the freezing cold air in a section of employee parking and Derek climbed into a huge pickup, after which, Mitchell and Jake lifted her into the back of the truck where Derek was waiting to buckle her in, tuck a blanket around her, and hold her for the drive.

She didn't remember much about that. She'd cuddled up against him, happy to let him take control. She didn't care where they were going, only that she felt safe. She remembered being carried into a warm house and up some stairs. She remembered catching a glimpse of Claire's worried face and then nothing but Derek. Derek peeling her clothes off, treating her like she was breakable china. Derek tucking her into bed and pulling her into his arms, holding her.

And now? She blinked at the faint sunlight coming in through the window. For the second time in her life, she woke up in bed with Derek, and not for the reason she would have preferred. A hot night of steamy sex would have been preferable to the disaster her life had become.

Derek's soft breathing was a balm to her senses and she laid perfectly still for long minutes soaking him in, letting him rest. A glance at the clock on the bedside table showed it to be just after six. Early. Too early. His arm was draped over her waist and he was curled protectively around her back. A glance down revealed she was, once again, wearing one of his t-shirts, which suited her just fine. She liked feeling like she belonged to him, like he belonged to her. The intimacy of the moment was foreign, rare and totally addictive.

She could get used to this. Which was probably not the smartest thing to be thinking when someone had just tried to kill her. Her head ached, but not too bad. She'd had worse scrapes on a motorcycle. Her cheek felt bruised, but again, she'd face-planted often enough when she was learning to ride that the slight pain was of little concern.

What she did need was a shower. She could smell the hospital in her hair, that bleach and sanitizer smell, the smell of sickness. It was pretty much her least favorite smell in the world. Moving slowly, she rolled her legs out of bed and slid out from under Derek's arm. When she sat up, the room spun for a few seconds but that was it. A few deep breaths and her feet on the floor and things stopped moving.

The room was gorgeous, the walls hung with mountain scenes and horses. It had a log cabin feel, or one of those homes that should be in a mountain retreat showcase. And she knew, without asking that this had to be Jake's ranch, the place where the Walker brothers had grown up together after they were adopted. The place felt magical, secure. She could imagine a young Derek here with his brothers, laying down the law and bossing everyone around like a miniature drill sergeant.

She stood slowly to Derek's grumbling. "What are you doing?"

She could see the en suite bathroom just a few feet

away. And she damn sure was not going to ask Derek for help in there. "I'm going to the ladies room. Alone," she added when she heard rustling behind her.

"Fine. But yell if you need me."

She ignored him and made her way to the spacious bathroom. A granite countertop and sparkling white sink looked spotless. The room was decorated with copper cutouts of wildflowers and mountain peaks, the walls the palest blue she'd ever seen with fluffs of white splashed across them like wispy clouds. The sunken bathtub looked large enough for a soccer team and the shower had two heads and a bench seat wide enough for two. It was beautiful and homey and so unlike the rat-hole apartment she'd been staying in that it felt like being in a 5-star hotel. Even the bright white towels were thick and fluffy. When she lifted one to her nose it smelled like lavender.

The room was almost too nice to use. Sitting on the sparkling white toilet? Sacrilege. "This is ridiculous."

"Do you need me?" Derek's raised voice carried through the closed door.

"No. I'm fine," she called back quickly. The last thing she needed was for him to walk in on her taking care of business. With a chuckle, she finished up, washed her hands and took advantage of one of the two new toothbrushes that had been set out on the counter. She assumed that little touch had been Jake's wife, Claire and she was grateful. She inspected the bruise on her cheek and sighed. Not exactly attractive, but it could have been worse. The ridiculous chunk of white gauze an overzealous nurse had taped to her head had to go. She peeled that off and inspected the stitches beneath. But she couldn't see them. The actual stiches had to be deep. There was nothing on her skin to see but some butterfly bandages that covered the top. It would leave a scar, but she could cover it with her hair, and it was better than being dead.

She tossed the gauze in the trash and gently wiped her face with one of the washcloths. Once that was done, she eyed the large shower.

Yes. Yes. Yes. She wanted a shower. But that wasn't the only thing she wanted. She was tired of playing it safe. And if last night hadn't scared Derek off, she was beginning to hope, even believe that nothing would. The other thing last night had reminded her? Life was short. Too short to deny her feelings when it came to the hot hunk of man waiting for her in that bed.

She made her way to the shower, opened the glass door and turned on the water, letting it get nice and warm before making her way back to the door. She opened it to find a worried looking Derek standing on the other side.

"Are you all right? Do you need help?" He looked her up and down, all business. And that just wouldn't do.

Wrapping her hands around the hem of the black t-shirt she wore, she pulled it up over her head and tossed it on the floor. She stood before him in nothing but a pair of navy blue bikini panties covered in bright yellow polka dots. They weren't exactly Victoria's Secret lingerie, but they were cute, fun and Derek didn't seem to mind that she wasn't wearing a racy red thong. "I could use your help in the shower."

"Laura." He shook his head, but his eyes roamed her body like a starved man inspecting a feast. "I don't think this is a good idea. You're still hurt and I don't want…"

She had moved closer, her hands tracing the line of tattoos on his neck and shoulders, deciding which section she was going to kiss first. But his words froze her in place and she looked up at him. "Don't want what? Don't want me?"

12

He lifted his hands to cup her face and held her, looking down into her eyes without blinking. "I want you so much I can hardly breathe. But you're hurt and scared and I don't want to take advantage."

Sliding her hand down his chest, she moved lower until she cupped his hard length in her hand. At least he wasn't immune to her. Far from it. "I know what I want, Derek. And I'm tired of being scared."

"Scared of what? Of me?"

She nodded and stepped into his arms. "Yes." Using both hands now, she shoved his black boxer briefs down over his legs and kissed her way down his torso until she was kneeling before him and could take what she really wanted.

He staggered as she sucked his hard length into her mouth as deeply as she could. She didn't start slowly, she swallowed him down like she'd never get enough of him and worked his balls with one hand. Her other hand she used to gently scratch his rock hard abs and grab a handful of his tight ass.

God, he was perfect. So hot. So damn beautiful. She wanted him wild. She wanted to let him know how much he meant to her. Words? She was terrible with words. But she could show him how much she cared with her mouth, her hands, her body. She could worship him, love him, without speaking a single word.

"Fuck, Laura." His guttural response only encouraged her and she swirled her tongue around the head of his cock before sucking him harder, faster. He tried to pull away, but she held his balls to keep him in place so she could do what she wanted to do. He was going to lose control. He was going to come in her mouth and surrender to her. She wanted him. She wanted him to give her everything. She was greedy for it.

He exploded onto the back of her tongue seconds later with a guttural cry and she swallowed him down like candy. Looking up, she held him deep and watched the cords of his neck stretch. The look of pleasure across his face gave her everything.

When it was over, she kissed the tip of his cock and stood, leaving her panties in a small heap that fell off her ankles as she made her way to the shower. He watched her, his eyes glued to the sway of her breasts, the curve of her hips. She had a nice ass, had spent long hours on a motorcycle to get these curves.

Smiling at him, she stepped under the water and left the door open. She put her face into the spray and winced when the water hit the cut in her forehead. But even pain was welcome. She felt numb. Numb and cold and alone without Derek. The world had become a shell-shocked gray. The only time she felt alive was when she was with him.

She used the water to rinse her mouth, and to hide the tears her weary heart cried. Needing Derek Walker had never been part of her plan when she'd run from Vegas. But here she was, lost and afraid and the only thing keeping her from shattering into a million tiny pieces was him.

The silence was suffocating and she began to worry that she'd horribly miscalculated, made a terrible mistake. What if he didn't want her? What if he only wanted to be friends? He'd never done anything to make her think he'd reject her, but he hadn't exactly acted like a horny teenager either.

"Laura." Her name. That's all he had to say, and she melted. "Turn around."

She did. Derek stepped into the shower with her and pulled the door closed behind him. Hot water cascaded down on top of her head, running through her hair and down her back as he moved in what seemed like slow motion. His hands came to rest on her hips and he pulled her closer until her bare breasts were pressed to his chest.

He lowered his head and kissed her. She was expecting out of control and wild, but his touch felt different this time. Reverent. Deliberate. She clung to him, trembling. The moment felt too big, like standing on the edge of a cliff knowing she was going to fall.

She was in love. It was stupid and reckless and totally unlike her, but it was too late. He owned her heart and soul. Worse, she'd begun to trust him.

Tearing her lips from his, she backed up until her back touched the cool gray tile lining the shower walls and reached for him, trying to pull him closer. Rough and hard she could handle. A quick, dirty fucking in the shower with the hottest man she'd ever met.

Water hit his muscled shoulders and ran over his tattoos like rivers of black on top of his skin. She ached to lean forward and trace the pattern with her tongue, but that would take too long. He was hard again, ready to fill her. All she had to do was push him.

His dark eyes looked almost black as he towered over her in the shower. She lifted a leg to his hip, aligning his cock with her wet center. She was ready. She wanted him. Just like this. Right now.

He shook his head and lifted his arms so that his elbows rested on either side of her head, surrounding her with the sight and scent and heat of him. "Is this what you want, Laura? Hot and hard up against the wall?"

"Yes." And she wanted him to hurry, but she didn't say it. That was a given.

"I don't have a condom."

She wrapped her fingers around the hard length of him, used her grip to pull him closer. "I've been on birth control for years. We don't need a condom." When he didn't budge, just stared at her with those dark eyes that could see into her soul, she leaned forward and took his nipple into her mouth, tugging and teasing as his cock jumped in her hand. "I'm clean, Derek. I promise. Please."

Her head was starting to pound and she didn't want to lose the moment, this moment, with him.

When she lifted her face to his he was there, waiting. He claimed her mouth, the kiss long and unhurried, as if he had hours to devote just to kissing her. He was relentless, not in pushing her, but taming her, forcing her to wait. Finally she surrendered, let him set the pace, stopped trying to push his buttons.

But kissing him made strange things happen inside her body. She was still wet and aching, empty, eager for him to fill her, claim her for his own. But this was somehow more than just sex. It felt like belonging. Home. He felt like home.

When she thought she'd go mad if he didn't move, he did, lowering one hand to cup her wet heat for mere seconds before he explored her soft folds with his fingers and slipped two of them inside her.

Her legs gave out but he caught her as she cried out

in pleasure, so swollen and sensitive for his touch that she was on the edge of orgasm just from riding his fingers.

He kissed her until she stopped making noise, stealing her moans and whimpers from her and swallowing them down as his own. He played her body until one more touch would shatter her into a million pieces, then positioned his cock at her entrance and lifted her higher on the wall and held her pinned there as he entered her with one solid thrust.

Her world exploded, her inner muscles clamped down like a fist in spasm, squeezing and pulling him deeper. Before it was done he'd shifted, carrying her to the small bench seat. He sat and pulled her down on top of him, her back under the warm spray of the water as she slid down, taking more of him, her knees wide resting on the hard seat as she rode him, grinding down on him so that her clit hit the hard planes of his abdomen with every rise and fall.

His hands held her back, caressed her as if she were beautiful and desirable, as if she were perfect. Unable to resist, she lowered her lips to his neck and did what she'd dreamt of for weeks, tracing each and every line of the tattoo there with her tongue, kissing them with her lips, nipping at them with her teeth as the tension built in her body again, faster this time, hotter.

"Derek." She said his name like a prayer. She knew it, heard the need in her own voice, but couldn't hide from him. Not here. Not now.

"Say it again." She lifted her lips from his jaw and looked into his eyes.

"Derek."

His hands roamed her curves, found the round curves of her ass and pulled them apart, opened her up as he shifted beneath her, going deeper. She felt her eyes widen in shock seconds before they closed in pleasure.

"Open your eyes, Laura. I want you to say my name when you're coming. Only my name. Nothing else."

She ignored the command, kissing him instead. With a soft groan, he moved his hands to the top of her hips and pulled her body down on top of his, holding her sensitive clit over his body as he rubbed, moving her back and forth just enough to make her insane, his cock buried deep.

The orgasm came at her like a tidal wave with no warning. She couldn't focus, not even on a kiss. She dropped her forehead to his chest and gave him exactly what he wanted, chanting his name as her body exploded and he came inside her.

When it was over, he held her for long minutes before gently washing her everywhere. She was too tired or too replete to stand, so he settled her on the bench. He worked the soap into her hair and rinsed it. Added conditioner and rinsed that, too. She didn't protest, simply let him have his way as he washed her gently everywhere.

Half asleep, she watched as he washed his hot body down quickly before turning off the water and grabbing a couple towels. He was dry in about ten seconds flat, the towel around his hips the sexiest thing she'd ever seen. He took his time drying her gently, patting the water out of her hair as she let him take care of her. It felt good, too good to be real.

She reached for him where he knelt at her feet, drying her calves, and buried her hands in his glorious dark hair. "Derek."

He lifted his gaze to hers, the look in his eyes soft and hard to read. "What is it, babe?"

Babe? Had he just called her babe? She ignored that. "My head hurts." She didn't want to tell him, didn't want to admit it, but she had to concede she'd probably overdone things this time. "I need to lie down."

Without a word he lifted her in his arms and carried her back to bed. Once she was free from the towel and settled between the sheets, he tucked her in and picked up his phone. She felt sorry for whoever was on the other end of the call. It was early. She tried to grab his cell before he could ruin anyone's perfectly fine morning. "It's early Derek. Don't call anybody. They're probably sleeping."

He looked at her like she was insane. "Do you think I give a damn? You're the only thing that matters right now, Laura. The only thing."

That shocked her into silence as someone answered the phone. "It's Derek. Laura says her head hurts."

Whoever was on the other end of the line, and she'd bet money it was his doctor brother, Mitchell, said something that made Derek's cheeks turn pink. "I know, I know. I'm an asshole. Just tell me what to do now."

She reached for his hand and was relieved when his fingers tangled with hers.

"Thanks for nothing."

When he hung up, she couldn't help but smile at the grumpy look on his face. "What's wrong?"

"Mitchell says you can't take any pain killers in case the headache gets worse. You just have to suffer."

"That's it?" From the look on his face one would've thought the world was coming to an end.

"What do you mean that's it?" He set his phone on the nightstand and leaned over her, cupping her unhurt cheek. "That's everything. You're hurting and I can't help you."

God, he was too much. Just too much. She turned her head and kissed his palm. "I'm tired. That's all. And you can help me feel better."

"How?"

"Hold me." It was the most ridiculous request she'd ever made in her life, and she waited, almost wincing in anticipation of his reaction. But all he did was toss his towel on the floor and climb under the covers next to her. When he was settled, she curled into his arms and promptly went to sleep.

———

Derek watched his family gather around Laura and treat her like a princess. Which was perfect, and exactly what he wanted. Claire brought her tea with honey, Jessica shared her status as an invalid and was completely unashamed at propping her feet up on the couch, her swollen belly earning her the right to be pampered. All of his brothers were here, and their wives. The new additions to Mitchell's family, the Castillo bunch, were in attendance as well as Connor and a couple of Jake's ranch hands and their wives. Claire's parents had arrived along with Miss Bea and her magical chocolate peppermint muffins with marshmallow frosting in honor of the day. Jessica's father, the sperm donor, was suspiciously absent, but since neither Jessica nor her brother seemed to care, he didn't ask. He knew all about fucked up family dynamics.

It was Christmas, and everyone had gathered to celebrate. And Laura, his Laura, was practically glowing with a strange combination of happiness and grief. He realized he didn't know how long ago she'd lost her father. Hell, he didn't know much about her at all.

"You keep staring at her like that and we're all going to think you're in love."

13

The voice at his shoulder was soft and feminine, a sexy, sultry voice that sold millions of hit records for her new label and had stolen his youngest brother's heart. Erin, a petite blond, had her arm wrapped around Chance's waist, sipping on a glass of eggnog spiked with buttered rum.

Chance, the little bastard, didn't say a word, but the knowing grin on his face spoke volumes.

For once, Derek didn't care. "She's mine and I'm not letting her go."

Chance raised a brow. "Does she know that?"

Derek glanced over to the corner of the couch where she was wedged into the large cushions watching Erin's brother take a waltzing lesson from Miss Bea. Her smile was soft and she looked tired, but content to let the noise and chaos of the family gathered for Christmas flow around her. The house hadn't been full of joy and laughter like this since they were boys. Their mother pulled out all the stops at Christmas and invited half the town. It had felt just like this, loud and chaotic and wonderful.

"I'd forgotten what this felt like." He looked around once more before turning to see Chance's reaction. His youngest brother's smile was as bittersweet as Derek felt. "Yeah, mom would've loved this." He raised his own glass of eggnog toward Laura. "And she would've loved Laura."

Yes, his mother would have loved Laura with her flare for living out loud and taking chances.

"Presents! Presents!" Claire and Jessica started the chant, which the band Castillo quickly turned into an opportunity for a quick a cappella number. The tree was huge, at least ten feet tall and decorated with so many sparkly things Derek didn't even try to distinguish the individual ornaments. There weren't many gifts left as everyone had exchanged presents before coming over for dinner and drinks, but there was one gift under the tree with a giant gold and silver bow. He'd completely forgotten about it but Mitchell must have found it in his Jeep.

Claire pulled the gift free and tossed it to him. "Derek got one this year. Must have been a good boy."

As everyone booed that assessment, Laura started to get up from her chair. "No. Derek. You weren't supposed to open that—" When everyone went silent and stared, she blushed a pretty pink and sat back down.

Well, any chance of escaping this undetected had just evaporated as the nosy members of his family all turned to him with more than curious stares. Laura had her head buried behind her hands but she'd stopped protesting. Her reaction fascinated him and he couldn't wait to see what could have embarrassed her this much.

With a grin he pulled the bow free and opened the box to find a simple white envelope lying inside. He pulled it free and opened it, shocked at what he saw.

"Well?" Jessica shouted from across the living room.

Claire had her hands on top of her husband's, Jake's giant body behind her where he'd snaked his arms around her stomach and was holding her close. "Give it up, Derek. We're all dying here."

"Must be something good." Miss Bea added with a mischievous chuckle. Derek figured her spunk was the reason she was still alive and kicking.

He had to read the contents twice, unable to process what he saw.

Erin had no such problem. She leaned in and started reading aloud to the group. "Two weeks at the exclusive Pink Sand Resort in Islamadora, an all-expenses paid island paradise in the Florida Keys. Our resort features a luxurious spa as well as snorkeling, surfing lessons and a one of a kind dolphin experience."

Her voice faded as she raised her head. "Holy shit. Seriously? You bought him a vacation?"

"To the beach?" Chance added, looking confused.

Mitchell ruined the whole damn thing. "So, what did you get her, lover boy?"

Shit. He hadn't bought her a gift, but he had been thinking about something, toying with an idea that he knew was one part desperation and nine parts insane. But it felt right and he knew when the words settled around him like warm, melted caramel that he'd made the right decision. "A black Ducati 1200S, custom."

Laura's gasp made him smile. Oh, yeah. He knew the way to his woman's heart. "No, Derek. No! That's too much." She jumped to her feet buy swayed. Luckily Mitchell was a fast mover and standing close, next to Jessica who was right next to Laura on the couch. Derek was across the room with Laura in his arms in seconds. He tucked her close, arms wrapped around her as she regained her equilibrium.

"Hush. We'll talk about it later." They'd talk about a lot of things, like the bike, and these tickets to the beach. He would go, but only if she was by his side. He turned to Mitchell. "How long is this dizziness thing going to last?"

Mitchell shrugged. "No idea. A few days. Maybe a week. Maybe two."

"That's a shit answer, brother."

"Then stop getting her…riled up." Mitchell's raised eyebrow and innuendo was not lost on Derek.

"Stop it. I'm fine." Laura pushed at his chest.

"Well, I'm hungry." Jake's deep voice broke the tension in the room and everyone hurried to agree. They moved to the other room to feast and laugh and enjoy the day. Derek kept Laura close, made sure she ate, then took her upstairs to rest when he noticed her failing. He watched her constantly, afraid he would miss the signs, afraid her head injury was worse than the scans showed or that she wasn't telling him everything.

When he hovered at the end of the bed, she waved a sleepy hand to dismiss him. "Go. I'm fine. Go be with your family."

Ignoring her completely, he climbed onto the bed and pulled her back to his chest, wrapped her in his arms and held her as she drifted off to sleep. When her breathing slowed and he knew she was sleeping, he whispered, "You are my family."

He loved his brothers. He loved their new wives. But Laura was special. She was his and the thought of losing her terrified him.

A few hours later, a soft knock sounded at the door. He lifted his head as Jake stuck his head in the room. "Yo, man. Brandon's here."

"Thanks." Jake closed the door and Laura stirred in his arms.

"Brandon? Is that the boy you mentor?"

"Yeah. I invited him over a few weeks ago. He and his foster mom and his two foster brothers."

She smiled. "Okay. I can get up now. I feel better." She rolled over to face him and he let her because he wanted to kiss her. So he did. She melted into his arms with a soft sigh that would make him rock hard in seconds if he didn't stop.

He couldn't stop.

With a playful laugh she hit him on the shoulder. "You are so bad."

"Only for you, babe."

Her eyes clouded with emotion at the endearment but he couldn't take it back. "Let's go. Those poor kids are probably freaking out already. Do they know the rest of your family?"

"No."

"Gaaa! Let's go, big brother." They made their way downstairs to find the three boys huddled around a game system Jake had in his study. They all shouted greetings when Derek approached and tossed him a controller. When he sat down in the middle of them, asking if they'd had pie and sweets and enough to eat, Laura leaned against the door with a smile and watched the man she loved make three lost boys feel important again.

A few minutes later, Connor made his way to her side. "Hey, Laura."

"Connor." His smile was genuine so she answered in kind. Everyone around the Walker brothers seemed to be honest-to-god, kindhearted, caring people. It was like they lived in a bubble. A perfect, idyllic bubble. The image was so far from her own past that Laura felt like she was holding her breath, waiting for a giant needle to come down out of the sky and blow this whole thing up. Pop her delusions with a loud, shocking boom that would rock her to her core.

They both watched Derek play with his young guests for several minutes before Mitchell walked by, took one look and chuckled. "He just can't help himself, can he?"

Jake, who was sitting on the couch behind her shrugged. "Nope. It's in his DNA."

"What's in his DNA?" Both brothers looked at Derek with obvious loyalty in every line of their faces. Connor, too, looked almost in awe of Derek.

"Saving people."

Saving people.

Her bubble burst. Gone. A snap of the fingers and she was wrecked. Derek saved people and she was the worst mess he'd ever met. He wasn't into her. He didn't want her, not really. She was a charity case, someone who needed him, needed help. She was broken and he fixed broken things. It was *in his DNA.*

Her smile felt brittle as she nodded at Connor and Jake, pushed her way past Mitchell and walked up the stairs as calmly as she could. She still had her phone so she turned it back on and used her app to get a car. She frowned when she saw how much the ride was going to cost her, but she wasn't staying here another night with Derek. She couldn't do it, not when every second of every day she'd feel like a charity case. As soon as the trial was over, she wouldn't need him to protect her anymore and he'd get bored, move on, find the next damsel in distress.

Shit. She didn't even have any of her own clothes. She'd borrowed a few of Claire's things to get by but there was no helping that. She'd just have to make sure she got them back to Claire before she flew back to Vegas in two weeks.

The car would take twenty minutes to arrive, so Claire locked herself in the bathroom and tried not to cry. Crying made her head hurt. But staring at the shower hurt more, so she went back into the bedroom and lay down to wait. She stared at the ceiling, reliving every minute of the past few hours over and over in her mind.

She'd dropped to her knees and taken his cock into her mouth. What guy is going to say no to that? She'd been the one to pull him into the shower, putting her leg on his hip, begging him to fuck her. She'd even bought the stupid tickets to Key West and he hadn't even bothered to get her a gift. They'd spent hours at the mall buying things for the women in his family, his new sisters, even Miss Bea had been given a gift.

The Ducati? That piece of custom art at his shop? That motorcycle was worth thousands, ten times what would be a reasonable gift for a woman he'd only known a few weeks. Nothing added up except the truth.

He just wasn't that into her. She was available, needed his help and had been more than willing to sleep with him. He was a good guy, but he wasn't a saint. No sane man would have turned down what she'd offered him this morning, with no strings attached.

He'd never said he loved her. Hell, he'd never even said he had feelings for her at all. All he'd ever mentioned was protecting her, keeping her safe. And that just wasn't enough, not when she'd made the biggest mistake of her entire life by falling head over heels in love with him.

"I'm an idiot." When Claire, Erin and Jessica had huddled around her asking for details, making it sound like something special, they were just wishful thinking and Laura fed into the dream.

She had to get out of here. All the family togetherness downstairs would make her completely lose her shit. Her head hurt. Her body ached. Her cheek felt like Iron Man had punched her.

And none of it held a candle to the proverbial knife blade that stabbed her straight through the heart.

Her cell phone buzzed and she answered, assuring the driver that she'd be there in just a minute.

Looking around, she was actually stupid enough to use her cell phone to take photos of the bed with its mussed sheets and the bathroom where she'd been with Derek.

Pathetic? Probably. But she wanted to be able to

remember every detail of their time together. He might not be in love with her, but she loved him. She'd never, ever been with a man who made her feel half the things Derek could with just a kiss.

"Goodbye, Derek." She wiped a tear from her eye, grabbed her stuff and left fantasy land behind.

14

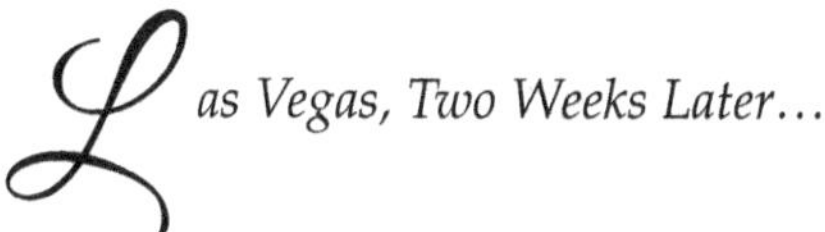

as Vegas, Two Weeks Later…

"WHERE IS SHE?" DEREK PACED THE HALLWAY OF THE Nevada courthouse, rage building in every step. Helpless anger boiling just beneath the surface of his skin as he waited, helpless, for the woman he loved to come stare down a murderer.

"The trial is scheduled to resume in ten minutes. I imagine they'll wait to bring her here until the very last minute." Chance pulled up the sleeve of his navy pinstripe suite and checked his watch. "I doubt they want her exposed to that asshole for a minute longer than necessary."

That was the truth. Every single minute was too long, in Derek's opinion. Laura had disappeared on him

Christmas day. She hadn't answered his calls or his texts with more than a brisk *I'm fine* or *I'm safe* or *don't worry about me.*

All of which helped him breathe, but none of it was good enough. She loved him. He'd seen it in her eyes. He'd felt it when they made love. And yes, that was a stupid romantic term, but he'd fucked other women. Nothing felt like touching her. Nothing else even came close. "Where is she?"

"Second verse, same as the first." Chance's rhythmic reply did nothing to calm Derek's nerves.

Why had she sneaked out like that? No note. Nothing. One minute he'd been holding her, the next? Gone. She'd vanished like a ghost, except his heart knew the truth, that she was real and she was out in the world hurting and alone and not letting him take care of her.

The long sterile hallways were built like an echo chamber, sure to intimidate anyone unlucky enough to need to be here. Voices carried but were muddled, as if the space was too big to hold them. The cold sterile tiles that lined the floors were huge, dark and sinister. He felt like he was in a damn morgue.

"I fucking hate this." Derek sat down on one of the hard wooden benches that lined the hall and ran his fingers through his hair.

Chance paced in front of him. There was absolutely nothing his little brother could do to help. Sure, he was a lawyer, but he wasn't licensed in Nevada and he had nothing to do with Laura's trial. All he was doing was keeping Derek sane. The legal mumbo-jumbo, all the language and terms and bullshit would have made Derek lose his shit. He only cared about one thing, finding Laura and making sure she never left him again.

She sharp tick of high heels had him lifting his head to the end of the hall. And there she was standing next to the prosecuting attorney and two armed officers bringing up the rear.

At least she had some protection, because the asshole waiting for her on the inside in his expensive black suit and tie looked three quarters certifiable.

He rose as they approached and when she finally lifted her gaze from the conversation she'd been having the attorney, she gasped when she saw him. "Derek. What are you doing here?"

The officers with her stepped forward but she waved them off. "It's okay. He's a friend."

A friend? Was that how she wanted to play this? That word twisted something dark and needy inside him, but he ignored the hurt that wanted to lash out at her. She looked incredible in a soft, cream colored skirt and jacket that made her look wholesome and innocent. No doubt, the look was part of their plan. Her hair was up in a twist with a few dark strands dangling over her face. She'd added a sweep of bangs to cover the scar he knew would still be fresh and pink on her forehead. The bruising on her face was either completely gone or covered with makeup. She looked stunning. Gorgeous. Perfectly put together.

She almost had him fooled, until Chance stepped up beside him and greeted her. "Hi Laura."

"Chance." She smiled at his brother and held out her hand. She shook like a leaf. The attorney excused himself, telling her she had about five minutes. The two officers split up, one going inside the courtroom, the other moving a few feet away to give them the illusion of privacy.

Derek didn't care. He didn't need privacy for this. He wanted the whole world to know he was in love with this woman.

Chance looked between them before squeezing Derek on the shoulder. "I'll be inside."

Derek nodded, his gaze never leaving Laura's as Chance disappeared behind the closed double doors.

Laura stood up straighter, clasped her hands together and looked at him. "What are you doing here, Derek?"

"I love you, Laura. Where else would I be?" He hadn't meant to blurt it out like that, but damn it, it had been almost two weeks since she'd disappeared on him and he hadn't been able to stop thinking about all the mistakes he'd made. Not telling her how he felt being the biggest.

She blinked slowly, as if he'd spoken in a foreign language. "What?"

"I said I love you, Laura. Where else would I be."

She shook her head. "Don't. I can't deal with this right now."

That was fair, and now he felt like an ass. He wasn't doing anything right. "I'm sorry. I just wanted you to know how I felt."

The door opened and the bailiff stuck his head out. "Miss George. You've been called to testify."

She nodded. "Of course. " He gaze locked on Derek's as she walked past and his chest filled with pride at her composure, her courage.

"I'll be here the whole time. We can talk after you bury this guy."

———

DEREK WAS HERE.

Why? What was he playing at? And why was he telling her he loved her? Why now? Her mind was focused on other things and she couldn't afford the distraction. She knew it, scolded her stupid heart for leaping into her throat when she saw him. But there was no stopping the foolish thing now. He was *here*. *For her.* Surely that had to mean something.

She was hanging on by a thread, her heart racing, adrenaline coursing through her. The shaking, half-terrified, half exhilarated feeling was one she was used to while riding or doing stunts, but not like this.

Normally, she'd be protected by leather and a helmet. Normally she'd feel the power of the machine she rode coursing through her, feeding her courage. But today she was exposed, her armor nothing more than a thin layer of cream-colored silk and high heels. She looked like a banker's wife, a soccer mom, the queen of the neighborhood bake sale…and she had to stare down a killer.

She'd much rather run him over with her motorcycle and call it a day.

She took the stand and swore her oath, proud that her voice didn't wobble or crack. The district attorney and his team had gone over the questions, what they would ask her, what the defense was likely to ask. She was prepared, and she stared Benny down when she recounted the moment he pulled the trigger to prove to herself that she could. Being a coward was not acceptable.

But isn't that exactly what you were when you ran out on Derek? The little nagging voice inside her head hadn't stopped tormenting her since the moment she'd fled. She'd taken her purse and gone straight to the airport, traded in her ticket and come back to Vegas.

Derek and Chance sat silently, Derek's gaze never leaving her face as she was forced to recount every detail over and over and over for hours. By the time the defense attorney was finished making her feel like a lying, drug addicted prostitute—none of which were true, but all were implied—she nearly burst into tears of relief when the judge told her she could step down.

She left the courtroom, walked straight out into the

hall and doubled over, her arms around her stomach to fight down the nausea rising to choke her. Benny was so vile, so evil, and she felt dirty now, like everything that stupid lawyer implied about her was true.

Months of stress, of keeping her cool were over and she felt like she was going to disintegrate into a million tiny little pieces.

"Come here, Laura." And just like that, Derek's arms were around her, holding her, keeping her together. She didn't talk, just collapsed into him, content to be in his arms as Chance stood nearby, watching the hallway, another protector.

"God, that was horrible." She shivered, her shaking almost uncontrollable, as if she were chilled and couldn't control the shaking in her muscles.

"It's over now."

"No, it's not." She shook her head. "I have to stay around until the trial is over in case they call me back to the stand. And then there could be an appeal, or a mistrial, or a dozen other stupid reasons I'll have to do this all over again."

His hand cupped the back of her neck, massaging the tension from her as he held her cheek to his chest. His steady heartbeat, his heat a soothing balm to her over-sensitive system. "What are you doing here, Derek?" She asked the question, but didn't pull away to hear the answer, simply stayed where she was, absorbing every ounce of him that she could get.

"I love you, Laura."

"You don't, Derek. It's a mistake. I was just a damsel in distress. That's all. In a few weeks, when this is over, you'll be ready to move on. I'm nobody, a stranger you've known a few weeks."

His fingers stilled in her hair and she wished she'd waited to bring this up. She wasn't ready to walk away from him again, not yet. She wasn't strong enough to let him go.

She expected him to pull away and scold her. Instead, he leaned down, swept her knees out from under her and carried her deeper into the hallway, to the recessed doorway of a courtroom that wasn't in use. He set her on her feet in the corner, out of sight of the rest of the world, and bracketed her head with his elbows like he'd done that day in the shower. "Want to run that by me again?"

"Derek." She wanted him too much to believe what he was saying was true. The risk was too big. He'd break her heart so badly it would never recover.

"Look me in the eye and tell me I'm a stranger. Tell me you don't love me, Laura."

Biting her lip, she looked him in the eye and couldn't lie. "I can't."

"Say it."

"What?"

"Tell me how you feel, Laura. Be brave. Tell me the truth. And trust me. Trust me, baby. Trust me to take care of you."

His whispered plea broke the damn on her emotions

and tears streamed silently down her cheeks as she stared into his eyes. They were dark, full of emotion, and utterly without mercy.

"I love you."

"No more running." He lifted his arm to wipe a tear away with the pad of his thumb.

"No more running," she agreed.

"Marry me, Laura. I love you, baby, so much it hurts. I want the whole world to know you're mine."

The moment he was done speaking, she blurted her answer. "Yes."

He kissed her, the gentle claiming turning violent with passion within seconds. God, she'd missed him. So much.

Behind him, Chance cleared his throat. "Hate to break up the party, but court's in recess until tomorrow.

Derek rested his forehead against hers, as out of breathe as she as he answered his brother. "You're going to need your own hotel room tonight."

Chance's laughter echoed through the hall as Derek escorted her out of the building and into her new life.

EPILOGUE

Islamadora, The Florida Keys, April

THE SAND WARMED HER FEET AND THE SUN HUNG LOW over the water in a brilliant display of pinks and oranges that cast a surreal glow over the people gathered. Palm trees hovered over the edge of the walking paths and tourists farther down the beach were packing up, ready to head inside.

Laura shook out her hair and smiled up at the man she loved as she walked down the makeshift aisle they'd carved in the sand. Her dress was white with a wispy, layered skirt that danced around her ankles in the ocean breeze. She'd left her hair down, the way Derek liked it, and carried a mixed bouquet of pink flowers. Derek was wearing casual pants and a white island shirt that made him look like a dashing and dangerous pirate. A sexy pirate. He'd let his hair grow the last few months, mostly, she suspected, because she loved to bury her hands in it when he made her lose control. Even more, she loved to run her fingers through it and caress him when they were relaxed and alone.

And soon, he'd be hers. Officially. Gold rings and the same last name. Her husband. Her lover. Her everything. The minister they'd hired to perform the ceremony waited as well. He was totally island, wearing white pants, a tropical shirt and sandals. But his signature was official. He could make Derek hers forever, so she didn't much care what he looked like.

The entire Walker family fanned out around them as she took Derek's hand and turned to face him. Erin and Chance. Jake and Claire. Mitchell and Jessica and their new baby, little Tommy, who had his dad's green eyes and his mother's auburn hair. He was chubby and cute and absolutely perfect, content to be held with his head down on his father's shoulder as his mother leaned into Mitchell's opposite side.

So much love. Laura wasn't quite sure where to put it all. Being around this family after so many years of fending for herself was almost like drowning, but it felt so good she didn't want it to ever stop.

Facing Derek, everything and everyone else faded into nothing. Nothing else mattered. "I love you."

He leaned down and pressed his forehead to hers. "I love you, too."

"Let's begin." The minister started the ceremony and the conviction in Derek's voice as he repeated his vows settled nerves she didn't know she'd had. When her turn came, her worries faded to nothing and she held Derek's gaze as she pledged her life to his without reservation. The past was the past. Forgotten. Derek was her future.

They exchanged rings but before the minister pronounced them man and wife, Derek interrupted. Reaching into his pocket, he pulled out an envelope. The once bright yellow faded around the edges.

Curious, she blinked in confusion and waited in stunned silence as his brothers came closer.

Fascinated by the strange byplay going on, she watched Derek pull a card from the envelope. He took a deep breath and Laura stepped closer as he began to tell her a story.

"My mom passed away about a year ago. But before she died, she thought up a crazy scheme to make sure her boys all found happiness."

"Worked for me." Chance blurted out, his arm around Erin's waist.

When she looked at Jake, he held her gaze for a minute and nodded. Mitchell was last, but by the time she got to him, she already knew the answer. Shocked that a woman could love her children so much, Laura turned back to Derek, intrigued.

"What's in your card?"

Derek tilted his head and raised his brows until she, and the rest of the family, settled back down. But when he spoke, he spoke directly to her.

"When we were young, about twelve or thirteen, she made each of us write down three things we wanted to do in life. Three dreams."

Wow. Laura liked her already, and wished she could have met the amazing woman who raised these men.

"But I didn't have three dreams, Laura. I only had one." He opened the card and folded it backward, revealing three large words scrawled across the entire right side of the card's interior in a sloppy, adolescent boy's handwriting. She read it aloud.

"Protect my family."

"Jesus, Derek." That was Mitchell, but Jake groaned and Chance, the youngest and she'd learned, the most carefree, laughed.

"No wonder you were always such a pain in the ass."

Derek ignored all of them, his gaze locked on hers. "I was afraid, Laura. Afraid to love them. Afraid to lose them. Afraid that they'd be taken from me the way my mother and my grandmother were." He paused and she reached for his hand, entwining their fingers, letting him know she was here, loving him. "I was afraid to love you, Laura. All my life, I've done everything in my power to protect my family, to make sure my brothers were all right."

His fingers laced through hers and squeezed. "And then I met you. And you terrified me. You were daring. Reckless. Courageous. You do everything full throttle and all I could do was watch you live life out loud and realize what a coward I'd been."

"No." Her protest died when he raised a finger and pressed them over her lips.

"But our mother was an incredible woman. And she understood. Somehow, she knew I'd get to this point, to this moment. And she wrote me a note that I want to read to you now."

The silence was profound, as if they'd entered a sacred space and tears formed in her eyes at the dedication and pure love the tough as nails men surrounding her were throwing off.

Derek lifted the card and read aloud.

FAMILY IS A STRANGE THING, DEREK. SOME FAMILIES ARE born, some are made, but there is always a beginning. And an end. You can't protect people, son. You can only love them. Love hard. Love so hard it hurts. Give your heart away and let it be broken. There are no second chances and no way to avoid pain. Live and know the pain is coming. But life is worth it. Love is worth the price. Live and laugh and hurt and cry. Be brave. Promise me, son. Promise me.

Love you forever, my sweet boy. ~ Mom

. . .

DEREK TUCKED THE CARD BACK INTO ITS FADED ENVELOPE and wiped a tear from the corner of his eye. When he lifted his gaze to hers, the pain she saw was staggering, but so was the love shining from his dark eyes. "I love you, Laura. I think I fell in love with you the moment I saw you. I want my mother and my brothers to know that I finally figured out what mom was talking about. And it's you, Laura. It's you and my brothers and this family. And if I die tomorrow," he stepped closer, lifting his hand to her cheek, "…or if you break my heart, I won't regret a single moment we spent together."

Laura glanced around the small group gathered in the sand and fought back her own tears. Sexy Derek was irresistible. Bossy Derek? Adorable. But the man standing before her now bared his soul as easily as breathing. His love was absolute. Fearless. And it broke down every barrier she had. Tears streamed freely down her cheeks and she didn't even try to stop them.

"I love you, Derek Walker. Forever."

Never breaking eye contact, he leaned forward and kissed her. His heart was in the kiss. His soul. Enough love to last a lifetime and she realized he was right. No matter what happened tomorrow, she'd trade a lifetime of tomorrows for this moment. For him.

The minister they'd hired cleared his throat. "Ah-hmm. It's not time for that yet."

Derek grinned against her lips and put his arms around her, deepening the kiss. Behind them, the rest of the family went crazy, yelling and whistling. Living.

Laughing. Loving without fear. Which would be the way she lived her life...*from this day forward, Derek, until death do us part.*

~ *READ ON FOR A PEEK AT AMANDA'S NEXT BOOK,* **Stealing Christmas...**

Zach:

Billionaire. Biker. Bad boy. That's what they call me.

Everyone assumes they know what I want in a woman. They're wrong.

Bethany Riley's hot-for-teacher glasses make me want to go back to school.

Too bad she's engaged, not to mention a soft, sweet, sensual woman like her would take one look at my tattoos, my leather, and run.

BOOKS BY AMANDA ADAMS

<u>The Walker Brothers</u>

Crash and Burn

Alone With You

Up All Night

Make Me Forget

<u>Magical Matchmaker Series</u>

Stealing Christmas (Magical Matchmaker, Book 1)

Billionaire's Obsession (Magical Matchmaker, Book 2)

<u>Other Books</u>

Claimed in Shadows (with Luna Davers)

Coming Soon from Amanda…

<u>*Sweet Mountain Mystery (Romance) Series*</u>

You can also find Amanda's books in German, French, Spanish and Italian.

VIP READER LIST

Sign up for my VIP Reader List!

http://bit.ly/AmandaNews

ABOUT THE AUTHOR

JOIN Amanda's VIP Reader List!
http://bit.ly/AmandaNews

Amanda Adams writes funny, sexy, new adult and contemporary romance, as well as a new YA romantic cozy mystery series. A full time author, Amanda spends her days trying to walk more and type less. If she eats a salad for lunch, she makes sure to reward herself with chocolate after (as any reasonable woman would do.) Her books are free of cheating--with a guaranteed HEA. Enjoy!

Connect with Amanda:
Facebook: http://bit.ly/AmandaAFacebook
Twitter: @amandaadamsauth
www.amandaadamsauthor.com